ERIC

AND THE

ANTI-TANKERS

ERIC

AND THE

ANTI-TANKERS

A Novella by
Joe Taylor

NAT 1 PUBLISHING
a literary nonprofit corporation
Books that make you question your choices.

ERIC AND THE ANTI-TANKERS
Copyright © 2024 by Joe Taylor
Produced by Nat 1 Publishing, a literary nonprofit
All rights reserved
www.nat1publishing.com
v.1: 11.08.2024

ISBN: 9798345422236

Cover, Design, and Edits by Weigel B.S.Roberts
Title Font: "Permanent Marker" by Font Diner
Interior Font: "EB Garamond 12" by Georg Duffner

For my faithful friends and readers, who made this book possible, Christin Loehr and Tricia Taylor

1. THE LABOR DAY PROBLEM.

After three years in power, The Pink Man took on "The Labor Day Problem." Labor Day's true vision, he proclaimed, had been hidden, purposely "obfisculated," in a dark, deep-state past. Now he revealed that its sure and true vision lay in celebrating business and business's benefit to the country. "Work, workers, work," he intoned, jutting the hinges of his jaw back and forth. Henceforth, he further proclaimed, on every Labor Day, employees should donate eight hours to their employer. Anyone not gainfully employed should scurry and freely volunteer to an employer of their free choice and freely donate that day's work. Who knows, he argued, but that they will thus find a happy occupation in commerce.

"Work," he sighed as if invoking eternal beneficence upon all listeners. Then he added, looking into cameras and jutting his lower jaw again, "This minimum wage law—" he stopped and shook his head sadly—"it's much too much of a burden on healthy corporations and small businesses. We need to rethink it. The market should be truly free. Work, workers, work!"

When Eric heard The Pink Man's proclamation, he stomped a foot and laughed. Then, just two weeks later, on the first Labor Day after this mandatory podcast's proclamation, Eric went wandering about the city, searching for a moral. His roaming had proven fortunate, for he was passing Darryl's Delectable Donut Depot when he heard a tank grinding up asphalt as it turned onto the street. Remembering the podcast, Eric halted his search for a moral and ripped part of his undershirt to begin cleaning the Donut Depot's display windows as the tank clanked to a stop beside him. Its commander debarked, sniffed at Eric as if the odor of unemployment clung to his armpits and hair, and then entered the donut shop.

"That guy out front work for you?" the commander asked.

"He's volunteering his day," Darryl replied, offering the commander a dozen delectable donuts. The commander took them and nodded, getting back into the tank, giving one last sniff at Eric.

Across this wide and so-glorious country, 9,323 scoffers and searchers of morals had not been so fortunate. Those folk had remained incredulous at The Pink Man's proclamation and had roamed the streets, insolently unemployed. A Labor Day "cleansing" took place that proved more effective than Tide Detergent. Next year when Labor Day rolled around, nearly no one was not volunteering to sweep floors, set mousetraps, count widgets, clean a toilet, or wipe down a storefront window. Eric himself busily swept in a Starbucks "magteria." The owner thanked him at day's end and gave Eric an old *New Yorker* to read plus a small coffee, black, no cream, no sugar.

2. ERIC'S HOME LIFE.

Eric volunteered at the same Starbucks on the following Labor Day also. You see, because Eric had majored in history and only minored in Computer Technology, he could not find employment. The history part posed a quote-unquote "major problem," for The Pink Man eschewed "pansy" liberal arts, flapping his hand loosely and squinching his face before cameras in what he took as the consummate effete liberal artist's pose. His supporters cheered and scratched themselves. The trickle-down mode had taken effect.

Through all this, Eric's parents let Eric keep his childhood room. In return, he mowed the lawn, took out the garbage, swept the floors, and did the shopping and dishes. Eric's Uncle Jim kept promising Eric that he had a neighbor named Willy Taylor who could get Eric on at the plant where Willy worked, but until that meeting might unfold, Eric remained jobless.

Then, after Eric's third post-college jobless year, Uncle Jim introduced Eric to Willy, who had—his uncle warned—recently lost his wife to an "unfortunate incident." Don't mention her, his uncle advised: he's trying to forget. Eric wondered why he would ever mention someone he did not know, and paced his parents' small backyard, searching, searching.

No moral appeared. He went back inside and decided to just be thankful that he didn't stumble over some false platitude lying beside his bed or craftily reaching for his ankle from under the dresser. He also decided to accept his uncle's advice. This was fortunate, for Willy got Eric on at the Blue Plant where Blue Things were manufactured. On his first day, a supervisor told Eric that Willy's wife had been set before a firing squad as an example to all anti-tankers and that Willy was undergoing counseling to forget. "Here's your station," the supervisor concluded, instructing Eric in his duties.

3. ANTI-EVERYTHING.

*W*ell then, what of these anti-tankers? Eric wondered as he walked home and paced his childhood room, once more searching out a moral, moral, moral. He looked out the window, thinking he'd spied one moving furtively in a bush under a tree, but it was only a hopping blue jay. So he returned to pondering the anti-tankers wandering the city's streets, leaning forward with their hands in their pockets to hide their agitation, keeping their eyes on the pavement to hide their single-minded hatred. They may as well wear a hinged electronic sandwich sign that digitally blinks, "Shoot me! I'm an anti-tanker!" Indeed, one November morning five of them had been yanked from this very city's streets, summarily tried and executed. Four died instantly, while one poor soul was left for an hour bleeding in agony.

"Something bit my armpit as I pulled the trigger," the fifth marksman said.

His comrades and the captain laughed. The captain walked to inspect the bleeding anti-tanker. "She won't be getting up," he commented. "We'll come back in an hour. Bullets are precious in these days of asperity."

But what was any of this to Eric? He was not anti-tanker. He was anti-everything. He looked out his window again. Nothing. No bird, no leaves, no breeze. And no moral.

Eric heard that the firing squad that November day had retired to a nearby Starbucks, where the Captain—a man named Carmel—bought four members of the squad Grande Coconut Mocha drinks and almond protein bars, while the fifth member, the one who'd been bitten by a flea and not scored an instant kill, was treated only to a medium roast coffee, small. No cream, no sugar, no skim milk.

After sulking for fifteen minutes while the others caroused and enjoyed their Grande drinks and protein bars, the fifth member complained, "I deserve better. I'm the one who left that rapscallion enemy of tanks to suffer as she should. Anti-tankers deserve to suffer, don't they?" The Captain and the four others thought this over and decided the fifth member was right. They all chipped in and bought him a Grande topped with whipped cream, three almond protein bars, and a fifty-Pinker gift certificate. Then they returned to the wall where they'd left the four dead and one dying anti-tanker. The wounded female anti-tanker was not there. It appeared someone had taken her away, perhaps to heal. Captain Carmel snatched the gift certificate from the flea-bitten marksman's shirt pocket.

On first hearing all this three months before, Eric had searched for a moral. He always searched for a moral.

4. THE ANTI-TANKERS' M.O.

The anti-tankers used modified Molotov cocktails, which they called Mollusk Cocktails. These weapons did not employ gasoline, which—being too volatile—exploded, thus not allowing the Super Express Glue concoction time to expand and congeal and immobilize the tank's cannon and sometimes even its treads. Hence, they employed not gasoline but diesel.

"In the good old days," one anti-tanker complained, "diesel fuel was cheaper than gasoline."

Another replied, "In the good old days, there was no need for anti-tankers."

"Ah, yes," another scoffed. "The world was lovely and brotherly and sisterly."

"We should be moving along," a fourth said, for the anti-tankers did not care to either maunder or ponder.

What the anti-tankers would do when moving is employ Nike Air Float sneakers to take the tanks by surprise, slipping weighted black socks over the tank's eight cameras. Then one agile anti-tanker would climb the turret and shimmy along the barrel to insert a six-foot, diesel-fuel-soaked length of Styrofoam into the barrel and light it, the heat serving as a catalyst for the Super Express Glue. If the tank were foolish enough to fire a shell, it would explode well within the cabin and kill all the crew. But most often, the crew realized they were snookered. They waited inside patiently, perhaps playing Uno or a round of poker, and looking forward to the plate of Oreos and gallon of icy cold milk the anti-tankers would always leave beside the hatch.

"You know," one agile anti-tanker beamed. "Inserting that tube is just like penetrating a nice and juicy cunt." This anti-tanker shifted her breasts unconsciously and smiled.

"Gross," one of her comrades commented.

The anti-tankers, you see, were too focused to be politically correct. They were too focused to be involved in romantic or sexual activities. Many were too focused to even be aware of their own sex. Some mistakenly tried marking fire hydrants or trees or Patriotic Pink Man posters, to become surprised they had to lift their legs so spectacularly high, pulling a muscle and cramping. Some sat on toilets and wiped themselves, surprised to find an intrusive appendage that did not seem to respond to their industrious wipes but remained stubbornly attached to their bodies, indeed, even elongating as they assiduously wiped.

"What? What?" They would hop up and exclaim, raising their eyebrows in fright, perhaps even fearing they were growing a tank's round turret and elongated barrel.

Eric had witnessed both of these occurrences many, many times. He'd laughed many, many times.

5. WHAT THE ANTI-TANKERS BELIEVED.

The anti-tankers believed that all tanks were inherently bad. They believed that all tanks needed to be incapacitated. They believed that once the complete destruction of all tanks was accomplished, the world would, in the words of an old, old song, return to its natural state, *The Big Rock Candy Mountain*. The anti-tankers were True Believers.

6. WHAT THE PINK MAN SUPPORTERS BELIEVED.

The Pink Man's supporters believed that all anti-tankers were inherently bad. They believed that all anti-tankers needed to be jailed or destroyed, preferably the latter. They believed that once the complete disassembling of all anti-tankers and the lubricating of all tanks were accomplished, the world would, in the words of an old, old song, return to its natural state, *The Big Rock Candy Mountain*. The Pink Man's supporters were True Believers.

7. ERIC HIMSELF.

Eric himself was a… he always hesitated to speak or even think this, but he supposed he was a true *dis*-believer. For sure, he often enough had conversations with anti-tankers, for being True Believers they were proselytizers. In the Starbucks magteria one glorious and sunny Saturday morning, he was asked by an attractive brunette anti-tanker if she might sit and share some thoughts with him, as she saw he was reading *The New Yorker*. (*The New Yorker* was adamantly anti-Pink Man, a stance that often enough caused paper or ink shortages at its printing facility. "Sorry, there was a wreck on the interstate." / "Sorry, eight cars were derailed on the railroad track." / "Sorry, the lunkers union went on a ten-hour strike." / "Sorry. "Sorry. "Sorry.")

At any rate, this brunette proselytizer took her cup of medium roast coffee black—no cream, no sugar, and no skim milk. She wiped a brunette wisp of hair from her brilliant blue right eye and the wisp crossed with Cupidic alacrity to her brilliant blue left eye, whereupon she sighed and let it remain. She then crossed her bare legs as she took a seat across from Eric. He could feel the heat from her knees on his when she talked, when she told him that he had a kind face she could trust and that "tanks were ruining the nation," and that "stopping them at all costs" was "fundamental to civilization's continuity." All this was typical enough of anti-tankers. Instead of easing in with the weather or the local sports team or the holiday season of the year, say Halloween or Christmas, they thrust forward with tanks, tanks, and ever more tanks.

Eric listened as her blue eyes gazed and the brunette wisp lifted to crisscross her so smooth brow. He listened for forty-five minutes. When he brushed her knuckles and asked if she'd like to go to the new movie, a romantic comedy starring Wanda Wonder and William Strong, she demurred.

"I can't. There is a meeting tonight. Would you like to come?" She rubbed her knuckles where he'd brushed them, uncertain what to do with that tingle. "We have meetings every night. We serve black coffee and Ceylon tea. It's black too. We don't use sugar because sugar is a precious ingredient in the Super Express Glue weapon that stills the tanks." She studied her knuckles. "Think it over. I may be back at dusk." She again looked at her knuckles. "You know, that was almost our secret handshake." She stood and walked out of the Starbucks.

Through the front window, Eric watched her cross the street, looking both ways two times. One and two, three and four. Very safety conscious, he thought. But when she hiked her leg incredibly high to piss on a Support Your Local Tanks poster, he realized her True Believer purpose lay not in traffic safety but in assuring a covert action. She grabbed her leg from a charley horse and hobbled off. Eric didn't even laugh. He realized that he, too, hated tanks, but for an entirely different reason.

8. THE PINK MAN.

Many times at arrests or executions of anti-tankers, when the number reached well into double digits, The Pink Man showed. The Pink Man's name was eponymous, for not only was his skin coloring amazingly pink, but he wore flaming pink shirts and ties under a rose-colored suit of matching trousers and jacket. Whenever The Pink Man smiled, his teeth showed oddly small for his mouth, and they spaced themselves somehow crookedly. Surely The Pink Man could afford cosmetic dental care. The rumor was that he wanted askew teeth to prove that he was of the folk. His shifting beady eyes, however, gave the lie to that possibility.

The Pink Man would appear, as if from a science-fiction teleport machine, and look about with those beady eyes. Some folk would instantly try to flee; some would stare in wide-eyed adulation. All nearby would stay at risk, however. Eric's new co-worker, Willy Taylor, said that his wife had been shopping for shoes when The Pink Man made appearance. Formerly, she had joined and donated to one of the many Pink Man clubs, the Sisterly Order of Pink Man. She had donated steadily for lots of years, ever since The Pink Man had ascended to office. By certified mail, she had received an embossed Pink card, though she rarely carried it. Perhaps, Willy often mused, matters would have gone better had she carried that card, and had she not been trying on Nike tennis shoes.

She was caught in an anti-anti-tanker search-and-destroy mission, she was summarily tried outside a nearby fabric shop, she was stood against a low building's wall and shot, along with forty-three others. No fleas bit these marksmen, five machine gunners. Two of Willy's three children became anti-tankers the very next day. He had not heard from them since. As required by law, moral rectitude, and self-preservation, Willy and the single remaining youngest progeny forgot the wife's/mother's name. A grief counselor had helped Willy and his remaining progeny in this healthy matter. *Grief-Relief* was the name of her clinic. *Donations encouraged.*

"She was pretty nice," Willy told Eric over a caramel latte Grande.

"Your wife?" Willy asked.

"Yeah, her too. I was talking about the grief counselor. She got me out of that bad Loop. My wife—" Willy raised his eyes to search the ceiling. "My wife cooked us all French toast every Saturday. Or was it Sunday? I forget. You know, it may have been just last year that my wife left. Maybe this very month or day. I'm not sure, I forget. That's how you avoid Loops. Forgetting."

"Forgetting?" Eric asked.

"Exactly."

After the execution of Willy's wife and the others, The Pink Man was to announce in a live news podcast early the next morning that forty-four very nasty people had been decommissioned from their evil tasks the evening before. "Seventy-eight," he said instead, studying a note before him, tilting it for realism's sake, and gave a grin with his crooked, of-the-people teeth. "Just yesterday evening."

"Excuse me, sir, but I thought there were forty-four."

A staff member photographed the reporter who'd questioned The Pink Man's pronouncement, and cameras followed her out the building for gait recognition.

9. An Incident.

Of course, not every citizen was an anti-tanker, just as every citizen did not align with pro-tankers or even with the various pro Pink Man clubs. Eric certainly was not foolish enough to think he was unique in being anti-everything. Surely there were others. He sometimes wished they were as easy to spot as the anti-tankers so that he could share some shrimp scampi and a dark beer with them. But alas, that was not the case.

Nor was it always the case that anti-tankers could be easily spotted, even with expanding gait recognition. There was an incident out in a small borough of this very city where six tanks and their crews were taken by surprise and destroyed, despite the eight vigilant cameras operating on each tank, forty-eight in sum. It happened this way:

Pro-tankers would occasionally feel a need to show their gratitude and reverence toward tanks. They would dance in the streets, merrymaking with some brand of misspelled light beer, until they spotted a tank or tanks. Then they would festoon said tanks with garlands of barbecued potato chips and Doritos. Often enough, the smiling crew would emerge and share a few beers. But then, one Saturday evening, a group of anti-tankers masqueraded just so. Needless to say, the bottles of beer they held were Mollusk Cocktails. When the crews of the six tanks emerged, they were killed, and the tanks were crippled and destroyed. *Killed? Wait, where were the Oreos and icy cold milk,* people wondered.

Eric saw all this on a mandatory podcast. All citizens were required not only to watch this podcast but to take an online quiz afterward. Eric scored quite low on the quiz because he recognized the blue-eyed brunette who'd approached him in the Starbucks as she stood by a tank with a grimace, wiping away the wisp while her comrades kicked at the bodies of the crewmembers and hiked their legs on the crippled tanks. Eric focused on her image until his eyes teared. And then with just one cleansing blink, Eric forsook his anti-everything stance. Eric was in love.

10. SEARCH-AND-MEET.

He organized a search-and-meet mission, starting with the corner Starbucks magteria where he'd first encountered the brunette anti-tanker. He resolved that, if necessary, he would attend anti-tank meetings, just so he might stand near her and feel her body warmth, since it was an unseasonably chilly early summer.

"See?" Pink Man supporters insisted about this aberrant weather pattern. "This proves there's no global warming! Brrr, it's cold!"

And then, in Starbucks one early chilly evening after work at the Blue Plant, there she stood, not ten feet from him, blinking her wondrous blue eyes. Eric smiled but quickly realized that was the wrong approach. He lifted a *New Yorker* magazine in front of his face, shifting it about to catch her attention.

She was wearing a red sweater, which clashed with her blue eyes. But then, anti-tankers were not known for their clothing styles—another way that the authorities tracked them down, for the remainder of society was imitatively stylish, often girding garish pink apparel about their hips or necks or wrists. Some went for weeks without brushing their teeth, cultivating a fine yellow patina in order to imitate The Pink Man himself. Dentists were even offering "De-bracing," a six-month program of skewing teeth to slant against one another, Pink Man fashion. *Stylish is as stylish does,* Eric always assumed.

"My wife," Willy had noted one day over a coconut almond latte Grande in this very magteria, "I think she usually wore a pink sweater. If I remember, I think, pink. It was hot that afternoon, though, so she didn't wear it. She was pretty nice from what I remember. My counselor said that memory can be a Loop trap, so I forget." Eric had nodded and searched for a moral.

Eric now coughed in his comfy Starbucks chair. He pushed and scraped the table, he coughed and he tilted his *New Yorker* this way and that. The woman in the red sweater with the blue eyes and the wispy brunette hair finally noticed. She carried her medium dark roast without sugar over and asked if she might join him.

As hard as completing these next acts came to him, Eric nodded curtly, and then, avoiding any interfering pleasantry, he vehemently shook his copy of *The New Yorker* to exclaim, "These tanks!" Then, as she adjusted in her seat, he brushed her knuckles for good luck. That part wasn't hard to complete at all.

She launched a thirty-minute spiel about the evil of tanks. Her coffee turned lukewarm since she took no time for a sip. Eric volunteered to buy her another. She demurred, but on checking her red purse and finding it empty of cash reserves, acquiesced by bending down to the floor, placing her hand palm up, and saying, "My bottom line this evening is quite low."

When Eric came back from ordering a second hot coffee, he thought he caught a brief smile as he handed her the drink, though it could have been an elongated anti-tank twitch, not a smile.

"What's your name?" Eric asked before she could start in about tanks.

"Teresa." She sipped her coffee and winced. "Better too hot than cold," she said.

Eric tilted his head and squinted, searching for a sexual double-entendre. But no, that was not this Teresa's intent, for her brow raised in sudden anger, so harsh that it dislodged the enticing black wisp from over her left eye back to her right.

"Ridiculous," she hissed.

Eric looked through the window to see a couple taping pink carnations on the Support Your Local Tanks poster just across the street. This poster already had been replaced twice because of vandalism and pee since he'd noted it one month before. The couple stepped backward and leaned on one another in admiration of their work. Then they leaned to sniff one of the carnations, their bodies creating an upside-down V that Eric found...

"Disgusting," Teresa commented.

"Coffee double-sugar cake!" the barista shouted.

"Sugar is much too precious these suffering days." Teresa wiped the wisp from her right eye back to her left.

Outside, the couple completed a slight, reverent bow and quickly walked away, creating two I-beams now. Eric understood why. Defacing political posters was a federal crime, and who could ever tell what some zealous Pink Man operative might consider as defacing? Those taped pink carnations—might they not represent an ironic, convoluted, and angry thrust against tanks? Might they not even obfisculate the poster's message?

"I'll be right back," Teresa said, standing. "Please watch my purse."

Eric nodded. Her hips were at his eye level now. Was she Mata Hari? He watched her hips walk out the door. He watched her head turn right, then left, then right, then left again. He saw her hand reach to move her brunette wisp from over one blue eye to over another. He knew where she was heading this time. And sure enough, she once more returned with a Charley horse in her left leg. Eric offered to massage it so that she "might repeat a command performance later."

She actually did smile this time.

II. Toward the Theater

There's no meeting tonight." Leaning to whisper, Teresa informed Eric that the anti-tank meeting that night had been cancelled because of a rumor of an imminent Pink Man raid.

Eric suggested the romantic comedy with Wanda Wonder and William Strong, since this was its last week at the theaters.

"How about *My Brother, My Sister*?" Teresa countered. "The director and the lead actress were assassinated two days before the first public screening."

"I thought they died from mixing cocaine and barbiturates and alcohol."

"That's the fake news story. Hollywood folk know how to use drugs wisely. Trust me, they were assassinated. The film carries a covert anti-Pink Man message." Teresa pursed her lips, which Eric had been studying. Through those lovely pursed lips, she asked, "Why do you think tanks are always outside those theaters that show it?"

"Tanks are outside every theater," Eric answered. It was true. Any event that might attract a crowd of fifty or more seemed to entice a tank's presence. Teresa moved the brunette wisp back to her right eye. Or was it her left? Eric rethought matters. "You're right," he said. "I have noticed tanks outside the Ben Ali theater where it's showing." With a sly dip of his head, Eric asked, "Do you think it's safe for us to go there?"

Teresa's breasts rose at this. Eric's eyes lifted in empathetic synchronicity. "One must be willing to sacrifice for the cause," Teresa pronounced, raising her head bravely. She may even have jutted her jaw just a bit.

When they arrived at the Ben Ali theater—just five short blocks away, and somewhere in each block, usually before the dead middle, Eric had made certain to brush Teresa's knuckles—when they arrived, there was no tank in front.

"Where's the tank tonight?" Eric asked the teenager collecting money for tickets.

"How the hell am I supposed to know? It's over my pay grade! I make nine Pinkers an hour at this lousy job! You a reporter or something? Have stock in tank manufacturing? Your turret and cannon in an uproar? Here's your damned tickets and change."

One thing for certain: the teenager in the ticket booth was no new-fangled android.

Teresa leaned to whisper: "I'm betting it's circling the secret meeting place. What a no-surprise surprise it and all the other tanks will get."

As they walked into the theater, Eric wondered how secret the secret meeting place would be with 293 tanks circling it.

12. MY BROTHER, MY SISTER, ERIC'S MOVIE CRITIQUE.

The movie involved one actress and one actor, stolidly facing one another at a bare table, speaking stolid, stoic, well-formed arguments about life and its qualities, its drawbacks, its puzzles. Occasionally the movie's director would walk on scene and speak piously into the camera, filling the audience in on some back-story tidbit. Unlike the actors, this director would blink for realism's sake, much as The Pink Man tilted his fake notes for the same purpose. Okay, more than occasionally.

Eric could understand why the director was assassinated: he was a pompous ass. He reminded Eric of a college history teacher he'd had when history was still taught on campuses. These days, of course, it wasn't wise to let folk know you'd taken such a course, much less that you majored in it, so Eric had deep-filed that cameo of the professor strutting in front of the classroom, chest expanding, lips curling, brows lifting, head twitching upon enunciating every self-important sentence. The students constantly awaited the moment he would inflate like a helium-balloon and float to hit the ceiling, maybe bob his head against the overhead projector. This film's director resurrected that image crisply with his very first on-scene pronouncement:

"And here we can see that Evangeline's past, that is, her life under an oppressive, paterno-rannical household, comes boundulating to the surface with all its bitter, entangling, unexpected resolvments."

Had this man attended even one English class? Had he read even one book? Even, Eric pondered, *one graphic novel?*

There were ten more intrusions on the film, all in this vein. Since the two actors sat primly facing one another for nearly the entirety of the film—one break for fetching coffee and one for some nasty bathroom business to add dirty realism to the film—since they faced one another with such prim and deadly resolve, the director's intrusions came almost as a welcome change. Almost. The film spanned one hour and nineteen minutes—Eric had a stopwatch function on his cell phone that he instinctively used whenever faced with spaces of tedium—or ultra-tedium in this case. The director had evidently convinced the two actors that a) they should never touch; b) their voices should never modulate over or under five percent in either volume, pitch, or cadence; and c) their eyes should stare with merciless, boundless, blinkless logic. Eric figured that any accidental blinks had been left on the cutting room's floor, for he never spotted even one. One hour and nineteen blinkless minutes—exasperating.

13. My Brother, My Sister, Teresa's reaction.

I've never been so mad, so incensed!" Teresa clenched her fists and said this as they walked into the night's air. She jerked her head toward a sodium orange streetlight and screamed at it. "Did you see? Did you see? He was everywhere in the film! Everywhere!"

Eric thought she was talking about the director and agreed, cautiously adding that he did think those eleven appearances a bit much.

"The Pink Man! The Pink Man! Not the director! That was Giovanni's last brilliant touch! The Pink Man lurked everywhere, though he never showed on the screen. His absence summoned consummate, constructive, carnal, and cogent deconstruction."

Carnal? Eric wondered.

Anthony Giovanni was the director of *My Brother, My Sister*. The cocaine-barbiturate-vodka assassinated director.

"And did you notice that Angelina was wearing a pink cameo ring? Pink!"

Eric thought it was orange but filed that away with the history professor, leaving both images to float toward some mental ceiling.

"Oh, the majesty of it all!" Teresa danced under the same streetlight and accidentally bumped Eric, who felt a static spark. Or was that a Cupidic spark? Teresa didn't seem to notice either way.

"How about a nice dark beer and we can talk about the movie?"

"The film. It's so much better than a movie. And beer uses sugar in its processing. You know how I feel about sugar's usefulness elsewhere." Teresa covertly peeked around to confirm that no one had overheard.

Indeed, Eric did know. He pictured Teresa scooting over a turret, her lithe body then undulating, wriggling, squeezing, scooting, slithering, sliding, slickly and slenderly slipping, while her legs wrapped tightly about the rigid, elongated cannon's hard, straight barrel, while her lovely sneakered feet and her ten toes gripped it, and her long eight fingers, her two pressuring thumbs, and two soft palms—or was it her full lips?—yes, her full lips embraced and tightened along the six feet of slickened Styrofoam, ready to stealthily, steadily, sturdily, sweetly, savagely, simply, surreptitiously, seductively, serenely insert that lengthy Styrofoam into that torrid, turgid, tunneled, tuberous barrel, and then only then would she lithely squirm and shift to ease—with her softly smooth hand from her tightly hugging hip pocket—a red Bic lighter, and after just one single flick from her Bic and that impulsive but controlling thumb and those lovely, long, lithe fingers... poof! Splat! Explosion! Full carnal release!

Early season snowflakes brushed Eric's closed eyes. So time had moved along. Maybe The Pink Folk were right, maybe Global Warming was only a deep-state plot. He opened his eyes to see Teresa staring at him.

"Where were you?" she asked.

"Thinking about tank turrets and barrels," Eric answered with a blush.

"That's good, that's good. Tanks today, The Pink Man tomorrow."

"Can we meet tomorrow for coffee?" Eric asked.

Teresa smiled. She actually smiled. Didn't she?

14. ERIC AND WILLY TALK

After Willy Taylor got Eric hired on where he worked, they became friends. Eric confessed that he had been jobless since The Pink Man's ascent, for Eric's college transcripts revealed that he had majored in history. For one year, Eric complained to Willy, he'd pointed out to prospective employers that his was a double major: history and computer technology. "You know, sir, inserting chips and boards." / "You know, ma'am, pulling chips out with special non-conductive nylon tools." For another year, he'd argued that history was only a minor. For the last year he'd complained that it was a misprint on his university records. "That history's a mystery," he'd joke, trying to lighten matters. His quip elicited only frowns and curt waves of the hand toward the office door.

Willy smiled and offered this advice. "Forget it."

Still, with damnable history on his transcript, the job that Uncle Jim's friend Willy Taylor had managed to get Eric wasn't much of a job; it barely paid four Pinkers more than what the teenager at the ticket booth made. Eric's job was to watch a gauge. If the needle rose above 124, he was to turn a valve to the left. If the needle dipped below 97, he was to turn a valve to the right. Eric didn't understand why a computer couldn't handle that, but was informed that the burgeoning company's IT department allowed that it couldn't be done. Eric suppressed a smile, for he knew that the IT folk didn't want any distractions from playing the current video game rage, *Anti-tankers, Tanks, Blips and Blanks*. But he kept that smiley thought to himself, wadded in his left pocket as he placed his hand around the valve and imagined his paycheck.

"She was pretty nice." This came from Willy at lunch one day, talking about his wife. "You ought to marry. It's pretty nice. My boy, he'll be dating soon."

"Do you ever hear from your other son and daughter?"

Willy shook his head in confusion, scratching a bald spot. "You gotta avoid the Loop. I do remember that they were pretty nice. But now they're anti-tankers. Nobody ever hears from anti-tankers."

"I'm seeing one now."

"Seeing is all you will do."

They were in the company's cafeteria. Eric looked down at his non-GMO avocado-catfish hoagie. He peppered it with more hot sauce, shaking the jar vigorously. "We'll see."

"That's what I'm saying," Willy replied, taking the hot sauce from Willy's hand, brushing his knuckles as he did.

15. A Piece of the Manger.

Big news for the city: A foot-long sliver from the actual, honest, real, true manger of Christ Jesus was going to be displayed in just over two months, during the holidays. Maybe one of the popes—there were a pair of them at this point, one to handle ceremonial matters, and one to make political comments, which always materialized as mysterious and veiled as Delphic oracles or as generalized as daily astrology advice—maybe one of those popes was even going to appear. The two popes alternated months when they could speak *ex cathedra,* and a flight of cardinals pre-checked each pronouncement to ensure there was no contradiction between what the popes affirmed from month to month.

"Tanks." Teresa glowed as she sang out this word. "Think of all the tanks that will congregate in this part of the city."

She and Eric were walking the streets. It was early fall, but leaves were showing their gay colors.

"Kids," Eric replied. "There will also be a lot of innocent kids gawking at that foot long overgrown sacred splinter. You can't just—"

"One must be willing to sacrifice for the cause," Teresa said.

Eric didn't realize it, but his euphemism would catch on. The upcoming celebration soon came to be known as Sacred Splinter Day.

But before Sacred Splinter Day might arrive, Halloween was coming. Even as he sat across from Teresa, Eric pondered sticking his hands in his pockets, leaning perilously forward with his head to the ground, grimacing and grunting—masquerading as the pluperfect anti-tanker.

"I've been invited to a Halloween party, a big one on Temple Street." This is what he said instead, giving a grin.

"I'll think about it," Teresa replied, surprising him. "It would make a good opportunity for spreading the Word." She added this when she noted his raised eyebrows.

16. ERIC ATTENDS AN ANTI-TANKER MEETING.

O h, you're one of those," an ultra-thin woman sniffled at Eric when he put cream in his coffee.

Eric blinked. Surely cream wasn't an ingredient in Super Express Glue. Was this woman judging him for indulging beyond an acceptable Puritan diet? Hoping for support, he looked about for Teresa, but she was standing twenty feet off, angrily shaking her finger at a man, who in turn was angrily shaking his finger at her.

The ultra-thin woman by the coffee, tea, and purified water stand pulled a bright blue shawl about her birdcage shoulders, gave a second sniffle and upturn of her nose, and then strutted off. Eric spotted Teresa's still shaking finger and was heading toward it when screaming broke out elsewhere:

"We have to!"

"No, we don't!"

"We can!"

"No, we can't!"

"We must!"

"We shouldn't!"

A laughing man dressed in a pink suit carrying a "Tanks Is Grate!" sign climbed up a makeshift stage and was booed, even as he waddled in obvious exaggeration. Someone threw hot black coffee without cream or sugar on him. He howled and jumped off the stage. Devotees attending tonight's meeting obviously had moved beyond humor.

"We have to!"

"No, we don't!"

"We can!"

"No, we can't!"

"We must!"

"We shouldn't!"

Eric would find out later that this night marked The Great Tri-partite Schism. The anti-tankers were splitting into Anti-turreteers, Anti-tankers, and Peace Now! Assassins!

The Anti-turreteers wanted to intensify the mollusk cocktails and not only disable each tank with Super Express Glue in the cannon's barrel and over the tank's eight cameras, but douse the tank's air vents with Raid mosquito repellent to force the tank's crew to open the hatch and try to escape. Only to be incinerated with the real original product, Molotov cocktails.

The anti-tankers, however, wanted to stay the course with their Nike Air Float sneakers, the six-foot length of Styrofoam, the Mollusk cocktails, plus the Oreo cookies and cold milk.

The Peace Now! Assassins! were the most extreme. They wanted to extend a death campaign to any federal, state, or local government workers, including postal carriers and dogcatchers, inciting a Reign of Terror that would surely guarantee imminent and eminent peace. "Peace Now!" someone shouted. "Make it happen!" Then, one of its advocates demonstrated a new machine he'd invented: the portable Gill-o-teen. With it, a one hundred and six kilogram weight would rush downward, crushing the to-be-assassinated's windpipe, leaving that person suffocating and dying.

"I've already perfected it," he beamed. "On five Peace Now! Assassins! volunteers. After I added six kilograms, the last four twitched only three times. Those three twitches will deliver a spectacular message to the public and a clear, effective warning to the Pro Pink faction." Eric himself twitched and blinked three empathetic times. Volunteers? In his mind's eye, the history teacher bloated and floated toward the ceiling, his finger shaking with admonishments.

Eric, at last, found Teresa by the demolished coffee stand.

"This isn't our normal meeting," she told him as they left and a cup of Ceylon tea spattered the doorframe. Her pointer finger was still quivering spasmodically. Eric's own hand shook, for just before the stand was knocked over, he'd poured a last cup of coffee with double cream, dismaying the woman with the blue shawl wrapped about her birdcage self, leaving her fanning her face in near apoplexy.

17. THE STALKER

As Eric and Teresa left the meeting, shouts still rang from the building.
"We have to!"
"No, we don't!"
"We can!"
"No, we can't!"
"We must!"
"We shouldn't!"

Eric noted a middle-aged man in a dark suit leaning against a building, smoking a cigar. Policemen and troops always wore pink, but this could be an undercover operative, Eric worried. He pointed the man out, since the glowing tip of the cigar seemed to follow them as they walked down the street, like the accusing gaze of Pink Man posters. *Work, workers, work!*

"That's just my older brother Terry. He's a stalker. He follows me whenever he can, whenever he's not trying some case in court. He's also a lawyer."

"Should we go back and offer him some of my coffee? It's chilly out." Eric thought about global warming but kept that thought in his left pocket, near so many other repressed thoughts.

"He wouldn't drink it," Teresa replied. "He makes a conspicuous consumption point of quadruped spoons of sugar."

"Quadruped? Quad? Quadruple? As in lots of fours?"

"Quadruped's funnier, don't you think?"

Eric gave a blink and stumbled. Teresa had made a joke. Even a bad one was a notable change. He filed this thought in his shirt pocket, where he could retrieve it easily.

"Why does he follow you? Is he watching over you, does he want to protect you? Or does he—but he's your brother, so surely not—"

"He wants to convert me into the Great Fold."

Eric had read enough anti-tanker pamphlets to know that the Great Fold was the anti-tanker name for what in other periods would have been known as the Great Unwashed. That is, anyone dirty and common and ignorant enough to bull-headedly stand outside the current Grand Idea Fold, presently meaning the anti-tanker fold. Soon he would learn that vile number was to multiply since the anti-tanker tri-partite schism was about to go into full effect: witness a chair tossed through a window back at the meeting hall. A crash ensued, tables collapsed noisily, and more windows were broken as Eric and Teresa listened and watched from a nearby bakery's lights.

"We have to!" "No, we don't!" "We can!" "No, we can't!" "We must!" "We shouldn't!" was erupting into fisticuffs, howls, and belches. The perceived Great Fold was multiplying with near exponential vigor.

18. THE STALKER DESCENDS.

E ric had walked Teresa to her apartment and then returned to his home—a room, actually, since the job Willy'd gotten him was quite low-paying. The room had a tiny kitchenette with a single-eye hotplate and an even tinier refrigerator, which could hold one six-pack of dark beer and maybe a small pack of hot dogs and kraut. No shrimp scampi.

The glowing cigar had followed behind until Eric unlocked his door and entered. Even then, the cigar glowed out on the street. Eric watched it from the sole, dusty window until it finally moved away.

Two days later, over black late-afternoon coffee, Teresa informed him of the tripartite schism that had occurred two nights before at the very meeting they had attended. She and seven others were searching out a new, smaller meeting place, she told him. Though the anti-tanker faction still held the plurality of the membership, they had voted to find a new meeting facility, to wipe bad blood and memories away. The blood was literal, for many fights had broken out two nights back. Teresa said several ambulances had been summoned, and intimated that one had served as a hearse. At any rate, tonight was to be a Teresa-less night. Teresa left, leaning with intensity, not even hiking her leg on the Support Your Local Tanks poster. Eric stayed and drank his café au lait and then walked out.

"Excuse me."

Partially shrouded by the growing dusk, Eric looked up from the glowing cigar tip into the man's bright blue eyes. Teresa's brother.

"Terry?" Eric asked.

The man sighed and shook his head. "Thomas," he said. "Ever since Teresa joined the anti-tankers, she has confused my name." Since Teresa had called Eric "Errol," and even "Harold" quite a few times, he understood and nodded sadly. She was a focused True Believer.

The man named Thomas stepped from the doorway and grabbed Eric's left arm. "I think we have a common mission," he said, squeezing Eric's arm.

"Search and convert?" Eric asked.

The man named Thomas smiled. Eric realized how stunning Teresa would be if she could only smile. He'd seen hints—what, three, four times?

"How about search and modify," Thomas replied.

Now, it was Eric's turn to smile. The two of them went for some dark draught beers and shrimp scampi.

19. HALLOWEEN ON TEMPLE STREET.

Since you went to the meeting—I'm so sorry it ended in such disarray—since you went to it, I'll go to the Temple Street party with you."

"What are you going to wear?"

"Wear?" Teresa blinked in confusion. "Jeans and a blouse? A tee-shirt any color but pink?"

"No, no," Eric said. "It's a costume party. For Halloween." When Teresa leaned and her leg twitched as if she were going to hike it on a nearby trash bin, Eric continued, "Halloween. Remember? Trick or Treat?"

"Trick? Mollusk cocktails?" Teresa answered, her brows lifting and her blue eyes widening in fright. "That might be dangerous."

Eric laughed. Teresa pouted.

"Hey, are you ticklish?" Eric asked.

"Tickle?" she responded.

Eric quickly reached to tremolo his fingers over her ribs. She squirmed, though he thought he caught the hint of a smile. That smile might turn regal, given time.

"I know," Eric exclaimed. "You can go as the princess Scheherazade!"

"Who?"

"Aladdin. The thousand and one nights." Eric leaned craftily and brushed Teresa's knuckles. "Scheherazade was wise, very wise. She tricked the evil Pink Man who was going to kill her sister."

Thomas, Teresa's brother, had already bought the outfit, which Eric now handily carried in a package under his arm. Soon enough it was settled. Though Eric quietly bemoaned the veil that covered Teresa's blue eyes, the shimmering silken dress that revealed her lithe figure compensated. They tried high heels, but Teresa wobbled too perilously, so they reverted to sneakers that Eric painted red.

"It's awfully close to pink," Teresa fretted as they headed for Temple Street and the party.

Eric only grinned.

Eric knew several people at the party, including one of the main hosts, who gave Teresa a wide-eyed look of approval and pulled Eric aside with a bottle of Guinness. He showed Eric a college transcript, pulling it from his kangaroo suit. Like Eric, he had majored in the unmentionable and minored in computer technology. The transcript all but glowed under a faux Tiffany desk lamp. Maybe it did glow, Eric thought. Computer technology was listed thereupon as the friend's major. There was no minor listed. The transcript was embossed with the university's seal.

"Run your hand over that seal," Eric's friend said. When Eric did, his fingers tingled. "Four thousand Pinkers is all it cost," Eric's friend said. "I've already gotten a job—and you won't believe where."

Eric bit and asked where, his fingers still tingling.

"At the precinct police station, running silly simple programs and maintaining their computers and printers."

Eric gawked. *Police?* It was now his legs tingling, and they were ready to run. A good thing that Teresa was busy proselytizing by a refrigerator in the kitchen.

The friend's kangaroo arm grasped Eric. "Want me to put you in touch with this guy? There's another opening at the station. It pays fifty-three Pinkers an hour to start. Two short weeks and you'll have paid for the forgery."

His legs recovered so quickly and boldly that Eric nearly dropped his beer.

20. HALLOWEEN ON TEMPLE STREET, FURTHER THOUGHTS AND ACTIONS.

Teresa still stood by the refrigerator. Tanks, tanks, and more tanks, of course. Eric carried a white wine to her. He was drinking dark beer.

"Oh no, that uses sugar," Teresa said.

The woman she was talking with assured Teresa that was not so. "In fact, that wine's so dry it probably spews sugar out, leaves a residue in the barrel," the woman claimed.

Teresa examined the wine, holding it to a light. She sipped it and laughed.

When she did, the woman tilted her head. "You know, you look familiar. I think I saw you in a mandatory podcast."

Eric's eyes widened, and he searched for an exit for them both. Between this woman and his friend who worked at the police station, calamity loomed.

"Oh no," Teresa said, taking another sip and again tittering. "That was fake news. The Pro Tank Pinker Coalition put it out. One of my friends even thinks that Doritos may have subsidized it."

"Doritos!" Eric and the listening woman exclaimed together.

"Sure. You know, to show how irresistible their chips are. Entice a tank crew from its tank with just one Dorito! How yummy can you get?"

Eric and the listening woman nodded. It was so illogical that it seemed sensible. No deep-state conspiracy, but Madison Avenue shenanigans. Teresa laughed again, and this time Eric relaxed and paid note. *White wine. Dry white wine, yes.* He put that thought in his shirt pocket. *Yes.*

21. COLLUSION WITH THOMAS.

Oh sure," Thomas said. "She was a lush in high school, loads of fun, though even then she was something of an outsider. No homecoming/prom queen for my little sis. Dry white wine, eh? I'll keep you in supply. Hey, has she put her hand on the floor and told you about the bottom line?" When Eric nodded, envisioning her doing so in Starbucks,

Thomas commented, "That's her standard joke ever since she took an economics class in high school. How'd the party go otherwise?"

Eric told Teresa's brother about the podcast and Doritos.

"Pepsi did one of me," Thomas said. "Though you can never be certain who produces and releases what without a lot of research—more than I'm willing to invest. In the Pepsi podcast, I was dancing a Texas two-step and offering an ice-cold Pepsi to a tank commander and an anti-tanker. When the figure that was supposed to be me offered it, they stopped screaming at one another and both reached for the soda. Their hands touched. Boom! Fast-forward and they're walking down the aisle to be married, with Pepsi champagne overflowing the tables. Fake news. It's everywhere. There's no such thing as truth, said jesting Pilate, while performing an old-timey jitterbug in his toga." Thomas popped a shrimp scampi in his mouth and chased it with dark beer. "Say, I can help you with that fake diploma," he added. "Have it for you next week."

22. Eric's New Job.

The fake diploma came even sooner. Eric found it in his mailbox two days later. With it, he too would start working for the local police station.

At first Teresa was upset, but then, "A spy! You can be an informant!" She tossed her wisp of black hair across her forehead. "A fake employee!"

Eric followed the wisp's movement, looked into her blue eyes, and nodded with reluctance, but also joy.

At lunch on Eric's last day, Willy bought Eric a grass-fed, non-GMO bacon-Swiss-hamburger to celebrate. "You know, seven years ago, I had that job you've got now. Once, I let the gauge rise above 124 and nothing happened. And once I let it drop below 97 and…"

Eric leaned forward.

Willy grinned. "Nothing happened. It may be a fake job that you're quitting."

Eric raised his brow in perplexity. "A fake job?"

"Fake news, fake podcasts, fake diplomas—why not fake jobs?"

And why not fake employees, Eric thought.

He carried those thoughts home with him, uncertain where to store them. All of his shirt pockets were already burgeoning, and they itched. He sat on his new apartment's front porch and watched people walking past. Teresa and her committee were deciding betwixt two meeting places tonight. Eric wondered if one of the meeting places was fake. He wondered if the teenage boy walking by on the street outside with his perfectly acne-free skin a-glow was fake. A dog trotted by. Its bark sounded tinny. Was it a real dog? Or was it fake? Weren't they manufacturing dog-oids now?

23. THE FAKE EPIDEMIC.

Eric was supposed to report to the police station for orientation the next morning, so he knew he should get to bed early. But he went to sit on his porch late that night, his gaze followed the dog with the tinny bark as it lifted its hind leg to pee on a fire hydrant. The dog's pee looked suspiciously clear, not yellow. Was it really just excess machine oil? Would the fire hydrant actually spurt water if someone took a wrench and twisted its valve? Or would it just squeak out a rusty sigh? Was it a fake fire hydrant? Put there to give fake assurance? The teenage boy with his miraculous skin leaned stiffly to pet the dog. Was it a fake dog, leaning into a fake teenage boy?

The two stars overhead—were they just fake fluorescent lights shining through the smog for reassurance? Teresa and her brilliant blue eyes… were they fake? Was her cupidic black curl fake? Was… was *Teresa* fake?

A traffic light changed. Eric could hear it click in the night air. There were no cars around. A fake light. Eric walked inside as it clicked again. Could the night be fake? Could a great dome ease over the sky to bring darkness?

He stopped at the table and rubbed his fingers over his fake diploma. He felt like weeping but stayed dry, fearing he might discover that his very tears were fake.

24. ORIENTATION AT THE POLICE STATION.

When Eric reported to Precinct Eight's Police Station at seven in the morning, he was surprised at the height of the successive superintendents who oriented him. The shortest was six-foot-four, the tallest six-eight, maybe -nine. Eric was born in 2020 when pre-natal care was nearing full swing. Vitamins and minerals had resulted in an upward shift in the population's height. Eric himself stood a smidge over six-foot-two. Then, in 2030, the Green-Life-First Party complained that these taller birth weights and heights squandered resources. They estimated that returning to what they dubbed "normalcy" could save 11.3% of the annual food consumption. The Tea and The Libertarian Cigarette Parties demurred since drug companies primarily backed them. The Hope-For-All Party had no issues with lowering birth weights and heights since they mostly represented impoverished families, and the average height of their constituents was five-foot-five. A coalition was formed, a compromise was reached: the drug companies could quadruple their prices on cancer drugs and, in turn, they would stop making pre-natal care available. Soon after this, The Pink Man took over. Coalitions, compromises, and parties became a moot point. "Yes sir" was the new norm.

So Eric was surprised at this display of height at Precinct Eight's Police Station.

"The primary thing you recruits should remember is…" The supervisor addressing Eric and the four others teetered. Eric wondered if she was sick or hung over. But she regained balance to complete her sentence. "Truth. Truth at all costs. That's our way here in Precinct Eight."

This was the opening speech given them. The newest recruits were then served cinnamon buns with extra goopy icing and coffee with triple cream and sugar.

The second man to address them, Lieutenant Riley, was six-foot six. "We take pride here at Precinct Eight, in giving our citizens unblemished, untarnished, unbefuddling Truth." He paused and teetered forward against the veneer podium. When he did, Eric caught a whiff of cinnamon. "Truth. Remember that, and you will go far." He clutched the podium and smiled brilliantly. It was as if his teeth were hooks reaching outward to tear into their flesh. But it was the man's pupils that captivated Eric. Each one bored like an electric drill, shaving flesh and thought away like so much soft wood to fall into spirals on the floor.

The third and the fourth to address them were also lieutenants, and they were also tall—six-foot four and six-foot five by Eric's estimate. Unlike The Pink Man's dentals, the teeth of all the previous speakers had been gleaming and even. These two lieutenants improved even on that, for their teeth glowed with fluorescence. Whenever they intoned the word "Truth," Eric thought he espied a gleam emitting from their mouths in something of a triumphant tidal wave. He attributed this to the excitement of the news that he and the four others were to receive an unexpected sign-up bonus of 900 Pinkers that very day. Was it just his perspective, or were these two lieutenants teetering forward as they announced this? And Lieutenant Riley's cinnamon seeping in the air, did it keep pressing, pressing throughout Eric's sinus cavities?

The last to address them was a woman. She was a captain and the tallest of the group, surely six-foot eight, perhaps even -nine. Eric and the others stared into her breasts as she spoke. Those breasts pointed forward sharply; they acted as a conductor's baton, emphasizing every mention of "Truth," "Honesty," and "Integrity." When the captain finished speaking, the breasts led her off the stage with sublime intent.

Precinct Eight was very upright, Eric decided as he received his bonus sign-up in eighteen crisp, new, fifty-Pinker bills.

As he walked out, he passed the captain's office. Through a small crack he could see her removing enormous lifts that were nearly stilts from under her gray, pink-striped pants. As he watched, she rubbed her tiny right foot. She then itched at her right breast, which wobbled loosely, disconnectedly from her body, almost falling into her lap. Behind, on her wall, a black poster with these pink words glowed out, "Truth will tell."

Eric looked about for a moral. Instead, he spotted a cinnamon twist wrapper on the floor.

25. A STROLL WITH TERESA, AN ENCOUNTER.

Eric insisted that Teresa meet him that night after his first-day orientation at the Precinct Eight Police Station, telling her he had important news, even though he didn't. But the fake height and the fake bosoms had left a misplaced quinsy in his stomach, so what he really had was a sunspot hot desire for something, just one simple thing that might satisfy him as real. He grabbed Teresa's hand as they walked, to test if she were a fake Teresa, maybe some new-fangled android black coffee drinker, or maybe in case she wobbled over the curbs they encountered because of hidden stilts under her yoga pants. But from the moment he grabbed her hand she stiffened and started talking about tanks, so he relaxed, he smiled. And her hand quivered uncertainly as he continued to hold it. This made him smile even more, for she was the real thing, all right. As they walked, she tilted her head to ponder their joined hands, and she nearly slipped on a half-eaten Big Mac on the sidewalk. Eric finally released her hand. Yes, yes, yes. She was the real thing, all right.

Thirty feet ahead, under a streetlight, a gaudy rainbow of motion and noise caught their attention.

"It's anti-tankers!" Teresa exclaimed, standing on her toes. "They're performing the Vitality Dance!"

"Dancing? I didn't think that anti-tankers went in for frivolity."

Teresa narrowed her blue eyes until they squeezed into coal. "Only on the surface is it frivolity. It's a rehearsal attack, but it's more than that. It's a spiritual code. There have to be ten dancers to perform it, just like with a Jewish minyan. Let's go watch. You'll see, Henry."

"Henry" was a new name. "Errol" had been Teresa's mainstay, with an occasional "Harold." Once or twice she even managed an "Eric." For some reason, her using that new, wrong name also comforted him tonight after his first day at Precinct Eight. Yes, yes, yes. This was a real Teresa, all right. They strolled forward, and Eric again brushed his fingers against Teresa's own. She looked at him and her eyes showed blue once more.

Teresa and Eric stopped. As Teresa predicted, there were ten figures dancing, just a storefront away, kicking their twenty legs quite high. Eric felt Teresa twitch as their legs kicked out, felt her shoulder bumping his own. Looking ahead while also watching her, he surmised this so-called dance was part of their practice for marking and defacing Pink Man and Support Your Local Tanks posters, as their legs went higher and higher, and their arms swung wildly as if to clutch the night air for support.

They began to sing,

> O join the chaos dance!
> O give chaos a chance!
> Lift your legs and prance!
> It's better than romance!
> Don't let us escape your glance!
> Come on, join us on the branch!

Eric squirmed with the last weird off-rhyme. The branch? As in a tree? As in a union local? As in a watering hole? He could do better easily: *Come on and take a stance,* for instance. Even, *Don't leave chaos to happenstance* carried a nicely odd ring.

And it rhymed. But maybe not rhyming correctly was the point? He turned to ask Teresa, but she had moved ahead to join in the dance to make it… no, not eleven. There were still only ten. He counted on his fingers to make certain. Maybe instead of a minyan they should call it a Bunyan, since in their minds they were chopping down tanks and posters.

Looking to a nearby corner, Eric thought he saw the eleventh. No, it was the glow of a cigar. And over there, on the opposite corner, stood what appeared to be a man in a kangaroo suit, shuffling in the early November cold. Where had the eleventh dancer gone? Only darkness bumped itself in the distance before and behind Eric. Could it be that even simple arithmetic was fake?

Teresa yelped. She hobbled to the side and leaned against a brick building with a charley horse from kicking her leg. Eric rushed over, holding his tongue about warm-up stretches. When he looked up while rubbing her leg, there were once more ten dancers under the two streetlights.

The tenth one looked familiar, like one of the taller policemen who oriented them earlier today. Eric narrowed his eyes to ascertain that it indeed was the one called Lieutenant Riley, the one who had teetered but smiled so brilliantly. Eric looked away as the dancing continued on, wildly, without any form—if anything becoming increasingly frenzied. Lieutenant Riley seemed to shuffle aside now and then. Eric wondered if he should warn Teresa. But even shuffling to the side, Lieutenant Riley danced so exuberantly, so extravagantly, and his breath huffed out such great shovels full of sincere cinnamon steam into the cold night air that surely… Surely what? Eric wondered. In a fake world, did the word "surely" convey any meaning?

26. FOUR WARNINGS.

After fifteen minutes, Teresa and Eric walked away from the Vitality Dance, Teresa still limping from her pulled muscle. Sequentially, four different people approached them from different alleys and store entrances.

"The manger means danger." This first warning came from the dancer that Eric recognized as Lieutenant Riley. The man again wore lifts in his shoes and wobbled just as he had during the dance, and just as he had during the orientation. He repeated himself, though twisting the words about and prancing. "Danger, danger at the manger, manger," he intoned. "Don't say I didn't warn you." Then he danced off, wobbling once and regaining his balance against a municipal trash barrel. Eric glanced back: there were still a magical and spiritual ten dancers under the two streetlights.

Eric blinked and looked for a moral.

The second to approach them was the figure of the kangaroo. While it had a similar tear in the suit as Eric's friend's suit had, the voice seemed different, higher pitched, maybe either feminine or younger. "Avoid the sacred baby's sacred splinter at all costs," the person in the suit intoned. If Eric were a musician, he would have recognized that the notes alternated between F, G, and G#. It wasn't much of a tune.

Teresa put out her hand to touch the kangaroo's pelt, but the person in the suit skipped away. Nimbly away, so no lifts or stacked heels were involved.

Teresa's brother approached them next.

"Terry," Teresa said. "I saw you watching the Vitality Dance, leaning forward as if you wanted to join. It's spiritually uplifting, isn't it? It makes you want to join, doesn't it? Oh. Have you and Aaron met?"

Thomas and Eric shook hands. Then Thomas spoke: "Keep your distance from the Holy Manger spectacle. Both popes are coming. Tanks will be everywhere. Danger abounds. That splinter will do worse than splinter." Thomas handed Eric a cigar, and then, with a blink of his brilliant blue eyes that was visible despite the hummingly dim streetlight they stood under, he handed one to Teresa, too. "You're old enough now, sis. Have at it." He pulled a bottle of extra dry white wine from beneath his heavy coat and also gave it to Teresa, winking at Eric as he did so. Then his cigar glow backed away, bouncing to the beat of the dwindling Vitality Dance still active.

The dance dispersed abruptly. Only the skittering of a stray McDonald's wrapper scooting along the sidewalk disturbed the scene. Teresa eyed the cigar in her hand and the wine. Eric brushed her knuckles in what he hoped would finally be the correct manner of the secret handshake. He'd been trying combinations for over four months now. Teresa gave off a hint of a smile. Eric noted that her teeth were even more brilliant than the fluorescence of the police lieutenants at Precinct Eight.

"You should—" Eric started, to be interrupted by a fourth person, a stranger who emerged from the doorway of a closed donut shop. Inside, two workers lifted a rack of donuts from hot grease to place it on another rack to cool.

The workers froze with the rack mid-air and stared out the window at Eric, Teresa, and the stranger.

"Take heed of the warnings you've received. But also remember this: the Holy Manger splinter might just as well afford a bond of bliss and love. Take care, and search for bliss and love. Take care that the Manger does not become a casket."

27. A CONFESSION.

Teresa sipped from the wine as they walked homeward. She laughed and lit the cigar her brother had given her. "Thomas, always the joker," she said, puffing. Eric noted that she had used her brother's correct name. She surprised him even further by saying, "I have to make a confession." She stopped and actually brushed his knuckles.

He took a sip from the wine bottle. They were under a powerful streetlight that made Teresa's hair look blue. Eric wondered what color it turned his red mange.

"The truth is that I just keep books for the anti-tankers."

"Books?"

"Sure, everyone has to keep books. I don't mean a library to read. No one does that anymore. But everyone, even anti-tankers, have to watch the bottom line. We have 446 members. You know, the bottom line." She bent low and placed the back of her palm on the sidewalk. As Eric smiled, remembering how Thomas claimed this was her standby attempt at humor, she winced from her still-pulled muscle and wobbled upward with Eric's help. She looked into the streetlight's glare and then at Eric. "Well maybe not everyone. Maybe not the Peace Now! Assassins! They won't be around long enough to worry about any bottom line. Fourteen of them were shot and killed last night. They'd assassinated a postman delivering two-for-one pizza coupons. The neighborhood was incensed and took matters into its own hands. It's amazing how many weapons are hidden under couches and bedsprings, how many cartridges stay available to fill those weapons and stray bodies. I think there are only nineteen Peace Now! Assassins! left."

Teresa paused. A lanky brown dog strayed from the shadow of a Hallmark Card and Candle shop. It carried a white paper bag in its mouth. Eric wondered, *Another warning?* A handwritten or typed one this time? Maybe a greeting card that uses rhyme? *We must you now warn, about a coming future thorn, so from the manger stay shorn!* Or maybe, *Keep in the center, do not enter, the Sacred Splinter.* Or maybe an aromatic cinnamon FAX from Lieutenant Riley or even from the tall captain with her fake boobs and her elevator lifts and her sore feet?

The dog walked right up to both of them and spoke. "The nice folks in the donut shop thought you two looked hungry, so they sent these."

A fake dog, a dog-oid. Eric had seen them in pet shop windows, with signs hung around their necks saying, "I can talk! And wag my tail!" The Green-Life-First Party had been complaining for sixteen years that pets consumed too many resources, so American know-how had come up with dog-oids. The Green-Life-First Party's ultimate goal was to replace all consuming life with –oids. Fake life consumed much less, a few lithium batteries at most. Save the planet. Could they, Eric wondered sometimes at night, just make a fake planet?

The dog nudged Eric with the white bag, which Eric took and opened. Six glazed donuts, freshly pulled from a hot fryer and dipped. Eric could feel the warm grease emitting from them. "Two apiece," the dog continued. "Two were for that guy talking to you, but since he left, I'll gladly eat those."

"PuckPooch," Teresa said, bending to pet the dog. "Like the fairy in Shakespeare."

"So you do read," Eric answered. "Is that another bottom line?" He bent in imitation of Teresa, not to pet the dog but to touch the sidewalk with the back of his hand. She smiled.

It didn't seem the case that PuckPooch was a dog-oid, for he gobbled both donuts. Dog-oids of course didn't eat; they just recharged. Moreover, PuckPooch had a conspicuous sexual organ, another trait dog-oids eschewed. He even snarfed down the second of Teresa's donuts after she realized they were made of sugar. She felt so guilty for eating the first that she had to hold Eric's hand for support as they walked toward his new apartment. "I don't think I can make it to mine. Can I sleep on the floor near your toilet? That's all I deserve for a bed after wasting all that sugar."

But once at Eric's, PuckPooch took that spot and proved unmovable. Eric figured he weighed over a hundred pounds. So Eric carried Teresa to his bed and placed her there, turning down the covers for her. He walked to the closet where there was a Star of Hope quilt that his mother had told him that her mother's mother's mother had made. Eric placed it over Teresa and hoped. From the bathroom by the toilet, he could hear the dog snoring loudly. It hadn't spoken since proclaiming it would eat the two extra donuts. Instead, it had gone on with doggie life just as if it were a real canine, not fake. Maybe ingesting sugar had convinced PuckPooch that it was indeed a dog, that canine was better.

Eric turned to watch Teresa, already asleep under the Star of Hope quilt.

Search and modify, her bother had said. Search and convert now seemed preferable. Eric lay down beside her, his heart and varied body parts casting hopeful rays to the ceiling.

28. BREAKFAST IN BED.

With daylight, the dog stuck its nose in Eric's right eye and nudged. "PuckPooch," Eric said/remembered.

The dog was drooling from its brown hound-dog chops, so Eric figured it was hungry. When PuckPooch's huge paw slapped twice at the bed, Eric stood, not wanting to awaken Teresa, who had been tossing restlessly beside him all night but now lay quiet and still. Had sugar guilt dampened her breathing? Was she a diabetic? PuckPooch nudged Eric's thigh, pushing him backward. With all that drool and that protruding pink schlong, maybe PuckPooch was real, not fake. Maybe the couple in the bakery had implanted a recording on its collar as a joke, and those were the spoken words Eric heard last night.

"You hungry?" Eric asked, raising his finger to quiet the dog. But surely it wouldn't speak at dawn's first light. PuckPooch whined and followed Eric to the kitchen.

Pancakes were off-limits because they used sugar. Teresa would never go for them; she was guilty enough from the one donut. So after making coffee, Eric fried some non-GMO sausage with three free-roaming brown-shelled chicken eggs. His new apartment even had a toaster, so Eric toasted three pieces of stale bread until they were crisp and new. He fed the dog and then he carried a tray into the bedroom for Teresa.

Who was not there.

She'd left a note:

Things a donut sugar-eater does not deserve:
  a.   *A warm bed and Star of Hope quilt*
  b.   *A good friend to help her into said bed*
  c.   *A funny PuckPoochie dog*

JOE TAYLOR

d.   Breakfast in bed

I'm going home to sleep by my toilet. Please pardon my vile sugar-mouth, my vile sugar-induced note. Donuts are the enemy. I am what I eat.

"Hurry, PuckPooch! Hurry!" Eric packed the breakfast he'd made and took it, PuckPooch, and himself out the door to run the eight blocks away to Teresa's apartment.

29. At Teresa's.

By the fourth block, both PuckPooch and Eric were panting. By the sixth Eric had to stop and catch his breath.

"You aren't one of those Peace Now! Assassins!, are you," an elderly man asked Eric. "You didn't steal that dog and murder a dog-catcher did you?"

"No, no! I'm taking my girlfriend breakfast in bed. She's depressed."

"That's a good fellow," the man said.

Eric sniffed cinnamon in the air and looked up. It was Lieutenant Riley in disguise, without his elevator shoes. The lieutenant wobbled off, stopping a young boy and girl, maybe ten years old at most, walking a French poodle. Eric heard the lieutenant ask them the same questions.

"We need to hurry, PuckPooch." Eric urged himself as much as the dog. Had the lieutenant recognized him? Would this affect his new job? The sun was rising. He had to be there in three hours.

They hurried on to Teresa's apartment house. Her apartment was on the first floor. Eric had walked her there several times after coffee and once after the Tri-partite Schism meeting. She had a blue mat with "I Heart Tanks!" embossed in gold. She'd told him that all anti-tankers kept these before their doors, both back and front, "and also side if they have those. It's our disguise. We wipe our feet on them. That's symbolic, you know."

Directly touching the blue I Heart Tanks mat on the concrete was a strip of black electrician's tape, over a foot long. PuckPooch sniffed at it. *Black, the bottom line everyone searches.* Teresa's voice echoed in Eric's mind. He peeled the tape and, sure enough, a key stuck to it. He opened Teresa's door, and he and PuckPooch walked in.

40

She lay in the bathroom by her toilet bowl. She tried to cover her legs, but her dress was stuck. Eric looked down: her legs had at least a dozen fresh small scratches and cuts on them. In her hand, she held a safety pin. He brushed back her black curl and took the safety pin away, placing it in the sink. She looked at him and PuckPooch.

"I don't deserve friends. I deserve pain. I ingested sugar."

"But you didn't know," Eric insisted.

"After the second bite, I did. I must have."

"You... we..." Eric looked to the big brown dog for help. PuckPooch licked one of Teresa's still-bleeding cuts, and she began to sob.

"Maybe we should get her out of here and into the living room," PuckPooch said.

"So you *are* a dog-oid."

"He's PuckPooch," Teresa said. "Canines are Truth, and Truth is Beauty. What more do we need to know?"

Eric pulled her up and walked her to the living room, situating her on a deeply maroon couch. He turned to fetch the breakfast he'd left by her TV, but it wasn't there. He searched on the floor.

"What are you looking for?"

"I left the breakfast that I'd cooked at my apartment by your TV. It's not there now." Eric looked accusingly at PuckPooch, but remembered the dog had been beside him watching Teresa and licking her legs the entire time. Now, PuckPooch was once more licking Teresa's cuts.

"Street people come in all the time and find something to eat," Teresa said. "I leave my key for them outside."

"But I..." Eric looked to see the front door partly open. He walked to it. Outside, sitting on a bench and eating Teresa's breakfast, sat a homeless man. Eric sniffed. That cinnamon cologne scent—the supposed homeless man was Lieutenant Riley in disguise!

Here now! Eric thought about yelling. For Lieutenant Riley surely made more than enough money to buy his own breakfast and then some. Even buckwheat-pecan pancakes and double almond latte grandes if he wanted. But instead of yelling, Eric closed the door and walked to pat Teresa's shoulder.

"I don't deserve to have a friend. I don't deserve breakfast," she mumbled.

It was too early for white wine. Eric texted Thomas.

30. WORK AT PRECINCT EIGHT.

E ric made it to work with only four minutes to spare. All the other recruits were drinking coffee and laughing. Camaraderie. They quieted when Eric walked in. Lieutenant Riley handed Eric a time card with a smirk. Had he recognized Eric? Had he really followed him to Teresa's and eaten her breakfast? Eric sniffed the air and the time card. Cinnamon.

At Teresa's apartment, Eric had found two packets of Quaker Instant Oats to cook. Spicing those with butter and black pepper and chipotle hot sauce, he spooned the cereal into Teresa's mouth. He even rubbed some butter on her legs to protect the wounds. He made Dunkin' Donuts coffee on her Keurig. He served it to her black and then made a cup to go for himself. He'd left PuckPooch with her, even though she protested that she didn't deserve to have her wounds licked. He had slipped to the bathroom and pocketed the safety pin in case she got any more ideas. He had opened her bathroom vanity and pocketed three more safety pins. Before he left, he actually kissed Teresa on the mouth. Her eyes had widened and she had shifted her black lock of hair about nervously across her forehead.

"When someone cares about someone, the someone who's cared about needs to take care of herself for the other someone, so that other someone doesn't feel bad. It's called—" What was it called, he had wondered.

"Love."

Had PuckPooch said that, or had Teresa?

Eric now pondered all this as Lieutenant Riley escorted them to their workstations. Eric kept an eye out for his friend from the Halloween party, the one in the kangaroo suit who'd tipped him off about the fake diplomas, but didn't see him. Maybe he worked a different shift. Or at a different group of workstations.

"Your job today is to search out Truth," Lieutenant Riley told them. "And then post it on Precinct Eight's website. We pride ourselves in posting first, so the other precincts must follow suit. Precinct Eight strives to be the Hub of Truth, especially now in preparation for the Holy Manger Splinter." And then Lieutenant Riley turned away, but not before he motioned to Eric to follow him.

When they were far enough away from the recruits, Lieutenant Riley took Eric's right arm and looked left, then right, and then left, then right again as if a parent teaching a child to cross a street. Or as if he were readying to piss on a

Support Your Local Tanks poster. The lieutenant had quite a grip, Eric noted, as his forearm tingled.

"Birds of a feather," the lieutenant hissed. He let go Eric's arm and walked out of the room.

Eric walked to his computer station and searched for Truth. As he did this, he also searched for a moral.

31. Work with the Bottom Line.

At her apartment the same day that Eric began searching for Truth at Precinct Eight, Teresa stood up from the couch and turned on her PC. Then she opened the anti-tankers' accounting program. She stood before the computer, entering the myriad numbers that had been emailed to her the previous night.

The anti-tankers' enrollment had swelled to over two thousand. Who knew why? Maybe because of the upcoming Sacred Splinter Holiday? Holidays made people want to join, didn't they? Or maybe because of the execution of the fourteen Peace Now! Assassins!? And there had been other executions also. Maybe because of them?

"I don't deserve to sit," she told PuckPooch.

Her computer dinged as it registered a new email. The subject line read, *To you.*

"I don't deserve emails from friends," she announced.

Nonetheless, she opened it.

"To the celestial and my soul's idol, the most beautified Teresa…" Teresa looked from the screen to PuckPooch and replied, "That's an ill phrase, a vile phrase." She saw that PuckPooch had taken a leather bound copy of Shakespeare off her shelf. It had belonged to her mother's mother's mother. Was PuckPooch reading it or eating it? PuckPooch gave out a whine and snarfle, so she turned to finish reading the email.

"I am at work here in Precinct Eight. My assignment is to search out the Truth and post it on the Precinct's website, as we are to be the 'Standard-bearers of Truth,' in our captain's and our several lieutenants' words. How, I ask myself, can I be such a standard-bearer when I deny a truth most close to my heart? So, I am writing to say that I love you, from my toenails to my topknot of red Scot-Irish hair. Did not our kiss just hours ago tell you the same? E."

Ernesto? She didn't know any Cubans. Ernie? Errol, like the old-time actor? Oh wait... Eric! Teresa fell back into a chair. PuckPooch forsook Shakespeare and trotted to lick at her wounds, but her trembling fingers stopped him, "I don't deserve to have my wounds cleaned."

32. Meeting Willy and Billy.

At lunch hour away from Precinct Eight, Eric arranged to meet Willy Taylor, remembering how Willy had been cured of the Loop that remembering his wife and two older children had caused. Willy, in turn, was sure his counselor could help Teresa, so they arranged a second meeting that night at the Starbucks magteria.

"I gotta bring my son. He's all I got left, I think. He's a good kid. No anti-tanker, no Pink Man, just pays attention to school."

"She's in a bad way." Eric shook his head. "I hope she doesn't scare your boy."

"His momma and big sister and brother done gone. Not much left to scare him. Besides, him and me went to that counselor I was telling you about, and now the Loop has been Loop-de-Looped from us both. The counselor, she'll fix your gal up, too. I guarantee."

And so, promptly at sunset, the five of them met. PuckPooch sat beside them because Teresa lied and told the barista he was a dog-oid. "A Service dog-oid," she added, showing the cuts on her left and right arm.

The barista made a face and backed away. "We'll have to sneak him any treats he gets," Teresa whispered to Eric.

Willy and Billy showed promptly. Billy was almost as tall as his dad, and he had the same mocha skin coloring. When Billy put out his hands to shake with Teresa, she said, "I don't deserve to shake hands with such a tall, handsome young man." She said the same thing to Willy, though he grasped her hand anyway and assured her that he knew just the person she should talk with.

When Billy wasn't reading a *Fantastic Four* comic book assigned for homework that night, he got along famously with PuckPooch and even taught him to bounce a tennis ball back with his nose.

"That comic book," Teresa asked, turning to Billy. "It doesn't have tanks in it, does it?"

"No way, no how, no diddle," Billy replied. "I gotta write a five-sentence essay about one of the people. I'm going to write about Sue Storm, the Invisible Woman."

"Invisible is good," Teresa said, searching about the café they sat in.

"I'm going to show how her invisibility and her psionic shields represent upstanding morals."

A moral? It was all Eric could do to keep from snatching the comic from Billy's hands and searching.

33. FREEDOM NOW! REVENGERS!

After news about the postman's death and all those unredeemed pizza coupons spread through the city, a counter-group emerged. They called themselves the Freedom Now! Revengers! These revengers hated anyone resembling an anti-tanker, no matter which faction. What the revengers would do is clomp about in Justin or Acme cowboy boots—preferably snake or armadillo or lizard skin—and kick each boot's pointy, steel-plated toes into buildings, walls, or people. The Freedom Now! Revengers! also used Super Express Glue, permanently adhering kicked, pale corpses or indented and dying Anti-tankers to the pavement, face-up or face-down didn't matter. The sanitation department found it easier to simply incinerate the bodies where they lay. Face-up or face-down.

Sugar was becoming outré citywide. The Fourth Estate, those indefatigable crusaders of Truth, speculated that sugarless days and nights might serve as a meeting ground for the three anti-tanker factions and the Freedom Now! Revengers! But it was a meeting that was never met, despite the fact that both sides sent info-bits concerning the many kilos of sugar consumed in creating Super Express Glue to the news outlets, vying to outdo one another in patriotism. Sugar was becoming so scarce and expensive that the donut shop where Eric and Teresa found PuckPooch had to change to biscuits and honey.

"The bottom line," Teresa quipped, bending outside the shop and looking at the displayed biscuits. Eric watched her bending. Her legs had healed nicely. Half an hour before, he'd convinced her to see a counselor, the one who Willy Taylor recommended, since she had so helped Willy and his remaining son to discard the Loop of the terrible past. Teresa's brother promised he would cover the cost.

34. WITH THE COUNSELOR.

"Avoid the Losing Loop! Shed the Perilous Past!" was this counselor's proud trademark.

The counselor's name was also Teresa. Both this Teresa and her secretary had green eyes, though, and both were anorexic at best. Neither could, in Eric's judgment, weigh much more than one hundred pounds. They were shedding much more than the past. Both Teresa the counselor and her secretary offered all the clients butter cookies, pecan sandies, and brownies with walnuts—all made with honey. And coffee or Ceylon tea, black or with cream. But no sweeteners, not even Stevia, because in its granular form, Stevia too much resembled sugar.

"Just like our meetings," Teresa whispered to Eric as the secretary relayed this dietary message and plied Eric with coffee. Eric could never turn down coffee. He had often searched for a moral to this fact but had yet to find one.

"I don't deserve to be served," Teresa insisted when the secretary offered her a drink or a honey snack.

Teresa the counselor's full name was Teresa Sigmund Jung, they soon learned. "No relation to either," she said after announcing her name and flitting from behind her desk to shake hands. "At least, I don't think so."

Teresa Jung had agreed to see both Teresa and Eric together. And when Eric mentioned PuckPooch, she'd commented, "Bring him too. I have honey-baked oregano-infused peanut butter dog biscuits."

She offered PuckPooch a dog biscuit. PuckPooch's nose quivered, and his torso shook.

"Is he a dog-oid?" Teresa the counselor asked, sniffing the biscuit herself.

"*That's* what I deserve," Teresa commented. And she leaned to take the biscuit away and munch it, making horrible faces. PuckPooch whined, Eric held his breath. Teresa the counselor inhaled deeply and shook her head knowingly.

"Tell me about your guilt," Teresa the counselor said, indicating a couch that would seat all three of them.

"I ate a donut made with... with sugar." Teresa held her stomach in pain at the simple memory of that donut. She repressed a gag.

"Loops," Teresa the counselor stated.

The three of them stared at her from the couch. She pulled up a chair in the middle of the floor, facing them. One of her high-heels slipped off and she wiggled five bony, thin toes. Eric thought he heard one toe give off a crack.

"Loops," she repeated, wriggling to get comfortable. "Memory Loops are what we all must avoid. They deaden our mental health. Take your memory donut for instance—" Teresa again gagged quietly, and Eric grabbed her hand while PuckPooch leaned into her side with a small whine. "I had a similar experience with pecan pie. I lied to myself. I told myself that the nuts were healthy, that they conveyed protein. This delusion came despite the cloying, sticky taste of the filling and that buttery sweet crust. I ate a whole, entire pie. I didn't even sit down at the table. I stood and I gobbled. After I finished that pie, I looked out to my driveway where my coal-efficient Pinkster convertible sat, just as if she were purring. All fuel is good, I told myself. All entities must have fuel. So I hopped in Pinkster and drove her to the closest Kroger where I bought four more pecan pies, all they had. And ten of those little ones they sell at the checkout line, just so I could munch them on the drive back.

"I repeated this for three days. My stomach distended. A woman at the checkout line looked at my tummy and asked when I was due, was it soon. "Protein," I answered. She moved into another line. On the fourth day, I felt Lazarus-like, Jesus-like, Buddha-like, Mohammed-like. Protein Power flowed through me, I believed. And I had yet to reach my thirtieth year! What would I be like at thirty-three? What powers would I wield in that pivotal, spiritual year?

"I drove to Kroger's and bought all the pecan pies they had, five this time. The little pies at the checkout line were sold out. This should have been a warning.

"Warnings are important to lift us from Loops." Teresa the counselor stopped and leaned forward, gazing at the trio on the couch. "Would you like more black coffee? Some honey-baked brownies? Even liquefied Stevia takes on the effect of sugar. That's why we must never drink it in hot tea or coffee. Did Anna, my secretary, tell you this?"

All three nodded, so she continued.

"Good. Now, back to the pecan pies. You see, what I came to realize later in my two-month regimen of computer-assisted self-examination was that pecan pies reminded me of a high school crush I had on a Cuban boy who jilted me. His name was—" she lifted her hand as if to swear in court— "his name I've obliterated so that it will never incite another Loop." She leaned back and looked at the ceiling, which held thin colorful ribbons, all shivering from the heating unit that just went on. "His skin tone was dark, his chuffy face was cratered with acne scars, and he had dyed his hair blonde. An ambulatory pecan pie if ever was one. Plus, he could recite the lyrics to *Guantanamera* in both Cuban and English to make you cry. And then he left me, in the middle of my senior year, just before a geology exam.

"So the attack came years later in Kroger's at the bakery counter when I stood before the pecan pies remembering him, silently calling his name, mouthing it, and feeling it on my tongue, cloying, cloying, cloying. A Loop had loomed right then and there, you see. And that loop brought on those four days and nights of how many torturous pecan pies.

"So now, honey is the way. No more acne-producing sugar. And I've substituted hazelnuts for pecans. We must harden ourselves against the past. Perhaps, Teresa, your mother, or your father—did they have pale complexions resembling processed sugar?" Teresa the counselor did not await an answer but continued. "Or perhaps you had a fluffy white Persian cat who ran out onto the highway to be brutally crushed by a roaring dump truck? Or a blonde Labradoodle? No matter the cause, you must rid yourself of this sugar Loop." Teresa the counselor paused. And how to do that, you wonder? Herewith is the moral…"

Eric straightened at this and leaned forward, holding his breath.

"You must purge, purge, purge. On the fourth day of my pecan pie-ness, I found myself at midnight, preparing for a fifth day, wanting only more. 'Protein,' I lied to myself, 'I must have ever more nut protein!' Of course, what I wanted was Cuba and *Guantanamera*. I ran out to Pinkster and drove her to the Kroger's. It was closed. I remembered an all-night Kroger's across town and drove to it. They had no pecan pies. They had no mini-pecan pies at the checkout lines. 'Is it a girl or boy,' a woman in the line asked me, drunkenly tapping my tummy. 'Is she due soon?' My stomach barely budged from her taps. I screamed and ran out to Pinkster. But Pinkster would not start. I had not fed her processor enough energy-efficient coal, being so busy feeding myself pecan pies." Teresa the counselor again looked at the ceiling. The heating unit was still blowing all the multi-colored ribbons. She jumped up and shouted, "Cast your eyes about you! Be aware of others. Be brave!" She slumped back into the chair. A knock sounded at the door. It was Teresa the counselor's secretary, Anna. "Ms. Jung, the time is up. You said to remind you." The secretary looked at the trio on the couch and smiled. "She gets carried off and away sometimes."

Teresa the counselor gave a limp wave of her hand to Teresa, Eric, and PuckPooch.

"If I have in any small way helped, please pay Anna on the way out. As I mentioned, that's our promise. You pay only if healing takes place. You may add a gratuity. We take credit cards, checks, insurance, and cash." With these words, Teresa the counselor's head tilted back to stare at the flowing ribbons on the ceiling. Eric looked to where she stared. She seemed to be fixated on three pink, intertwining ribbons.

The trio stood. When the counselor's office door shut, Teresa inhaled deeply. "Here I stand," she announced, "Pure and purged. I will never feel guilt again. I can do no other."

Eric and PuckPooch both tilted their heads toward her as if bookends.

Eric pulled out his billfold and paid the secretary with Thomas's cash.

"Will you be needing another appointment?" Anna the secretary asked.

Eric looked to Teresa, who was giddily smiling. "I don't think so," he said.

35. POSSIBLE PINK MAN PLANS: SACRED SPLINTER DAY AND THE SPECIAL NEEDS TURKEY.

All the news outlets and social media were agog. The entire Fourth Estate was all but dancing in the streets. Just three and a half weeks away! Not one, understand, but both popes visiting the city! Jews, Moslems, Hindus, Jains, Buddhists, Protestants, and Mormons invited! A spiritual hullaballoo!

All but the anti-tankers and their factions were invited. The Pink Man was going to speak. His crooked, yellow teeth were going to praise the Sacred Splinter. Many planned accordingly:

All the city's schools, both public and private, were given vacation—were given orders, actually—to attend the Sacred Splinter parade.

The special needs turkey that The Pink Man would soon enough pardon for Thanksgiving was to be headlined for the second festivity. It was rumored that The Pink Man himself would lead the happy pardoned turkey on a pink leash if certain security could be arranged.

Two shining, clean-coal burning popemobiles were to follow.

A convoy of one hundred and twenty-three other mobiles were to carry religious dignitaries and clerics from around the city, even from out of state, even from the whole world. Since The Pink Man had often voiced a fondness for the Easter Bunny, might not a large pink inflatable Bunny bob at the end of the parade, right before the Sacred Splinter? The length of the parade might take up four entire miles, security calculated. Nine, The Pink Man let slip in a podcast, tilting a note card. Maybe even eleven, he said, giving the card another tilt. Four times the length of the upcoming Macy's Day parade, which would also feature The Pink Man in a leading role. Maybe even two leading roles, ongoing rumors had it. Or more, for no one could ever get enough of The Pink Man. Thus was whispered. Thus said his aides and cabinet. Thus said The Pink Man himself.

There might be over a thousand tubas playing at the Sacred Splinter celebration. It was The Pink Man's favorite instrument, really the only musical instrument he cared for, truth be known. Well, maybe drums.

The Pink Man wanted to gather fifty suspected anti-tankers and have them lined against a wall and shot mid-parade while those tubas oompahed. "It will be the biggest and bestest execution yet!" The Pink Man suggested this in a meeting with his advisors, who at first advised that there would be many children there and that a public execution would shock their childish sensibilities.

The Pink Man countered that was precisely why the execution should take place—to bring the children into the world of realpolitik. "They'll be gnawing on turkey drumsticks just three weeks before, won't they? How innocent can they be? Besides, they'll get a kick out of it. We'll distribute candied caramel apples. Just before. Or maybe just after. Or maybe both." The Pink Man rubbed his little hands together and smiled, showing as many of his crooked teeth as he could. "The biggest and bestest yet. That's what we're going to have."

His advisors shook their heads. Then another advisor pointed out that there had already been a larger execution, the seventy-eight The Pink Man announced in the previous month, even though it was only forty-four. An aide took a picture of this advisor.

"One hundred then," The Pink Man replied, giving a nod of his head that the advisor who'd spoken should also be captured on film for gait recognition.

Plans coalesced.

Quietly, a round-up began. One by one, folk were snatched off the street. An elderly advisor to The Pink Man, angered because a great-grandchild had given him a bad cold from pre-school, suggested that a few youngsters should be sprinkled in the group just to drive the point home to the watching schoolchildren that no one was above the law. The Pink Man thought it over and agreed. "That's a grand idea. I'm glad I thought of it." The advisor sneezed, adjusted his pink tie, and smiled.

36. REFORMATION.

The anti-tankers had re-grouped, taking pity on the dwindling Peace Now! Assassins! and the confused Anti-turreteers, who had yet to destroy a tank crew because of internal squabbles over how to safely make the Molotov cocktails, despite eighteen different recipes on Google. "That's exactly the problem," one Anti-turreteer complained. "How are we supposed to know which recipe is true?"

Once more, Teresa was elected to head the search for a new meeting hall. She induced Eric to sit in on their committee as an outside specialist in electronics. "We're going to need closed circuit and big screens since our membership has grown so quickly."

"Exponentially," one anti-tanker added, raising three fingers. One was bandaged, Eric noted.

"Yes, exponentially," Teresa agreed. And she raised four fingers, all clean and un-bandaged. Eric sighed with relief. He'd thought she was going to stoop and demonstrate the bottom line, but she remained erect, those four fingers wriggling in the meeting room's air.

37. RAW FOOTAGE SEEPS OUT.

Special report! Raw, uncensored footage!
Thus, the teaser read for the podcast, which featured a wobbly, hand-held camera showing 144 girls, from ages eight to fourteen, emerging from a pizza parlor in the city, being released from a four-story underground dungeon where they'd been kept awaiting transfer to an ocean liner in international waters where they'd be impregnated and then aborted so that the fetuses could be used in Satanic ritual. All the girls were weeping wildly and ran to the arms of the police officers and Pink Man operatives who'd released

them. Eric thought that one of the men resembled Lieutenant Riley, though he couldn't be certain, for the sniff app on their home computer was broken.

38. Even More Raw Footage Seeps Out.

W *arning! The footage contains graphic material. Be advised before viewing!* "Patrons have long suspected Donna's Dunkin' Delights, for there was entirely too much nightly activity about her tiny shop," the erstwhile reporter reported, her face wide with shock.

Wobbly footage showed 144 boys, from ages six to sixteen, emerging from the donut shop where they'd been held in soundproof underground pods and tortured as part of an "interrogation experiment" sponsored by—and "this is not entirely confirmed yet," the blonde announcer whispered—"a splinter group of Pink Man fanatics wanting to cleanse the nation."

Eric again was not certain, but he thought that one of the anti-tankers who led the bleeding, bruised, confused, and weeping boys out from the donut shop resembled Lieutenant Riley. But he couldn't be sure since the Smellerator for the TV was broken and no hint of cinnamon lay about.

"Remind me to get a replacement Smellerator air drift accessory."

There was no response, for Teresa had taken PuckPooch for a bathroom walk, being certain to take her special electronic scoop tool that vaporized all the waste matter.

39. The Search for a New Hall.

W hat are you going to use this hall for?" the building's owner asked Teresa. Eric stiffened when she answered truthfully. He recalled the previous night's footage of tortured young boys and smacked his forehead. He had yet to order the replacement Smellerator air drifter accessory.

The owner smiled grandly. "That's the beauty about capitalism," the future landlord said, scratching his goatee. "It don't care. Widgets, assault rifles, atom bombs, anti-tankers, or cotton candy—go on and sell 'em all. It don't care."

Eric was proud of Teresa. She didn't even wince at the mention of cotton candy.

40. A PROBLEM AT PRECINCT EIGHT.

Whenever Eric wasn't inserting new memory boards, swapping out frayed wiring, or changing out batteries for Bluetooth keyboards, he was assigned to search for Truth. This came natural to him, since he really viewed this secondary job as his primary job: the Search for a Moral. It was a job he never left, which is why he discovered and watched those two podcasts at home nights before. In the past week at work, he'd deleted nineteen clips of Teresa moving her black curl while standing amid anti-tankers who were kicking the corpses of tank crews and hiking their legs on burning tanks.

And now there was a new one. It showed her eating a glazed donut and then hiking her leg on a Support Your Local Tank poster. Eric remembered that Thomas had told him of the fake Pepsi podcast. While Thomas might laugh it off, Teresa would surely fall back into a Loop—that is, if she lived and wasn't rounded up from face- or gait- or charley horse- or chewing-recognition. Rumor was that The Pink Man was covertly arresting anti-tankers and suspected anti-tankers for a mass execution on Turkey Day or maybe Sacred Splinter Day, the day the Most Holy Manger was to be unveiled, and both Popes were to offer a homily and a blessing, if not a carbon-14 test.

Eric texted Thomas about this spurious donut-eating, leg-hiking podcast. Thomas advised Eric to buy two bottles of hair dye for Teresa. *She's always envied redheads,* he texted back. *See if you can convince her to match your hair shade and go with that. Maybe she should gain some weight. Eat some glazed donuts. Just kidding, just kidding.*

Eric enlisted his friend in the kangaroo suit, the one who'd tipped him off about the fake diploma, to help purge any clips of Teresa from the Truth Files. He asked Willy Taylor and his son to keep their eyes out for podcasts that might have evaded him and made it to the Net.

Most importantly, Eric persuaded Teresa to go on a thirty-day diet called WeightAbate! This diet delivered, once a day, three meals and two healthy vegetable/fruit snacks. It was expensive, but Thomas promised to pay. While this certainly wouldn't add any pounds to Teresa, Eric and Thomas felt that eating in the apartment would ensure that Teresa's public exposure was kept to a minimum.

The night that Eric first convinced Teresa to follow this diet offered a scare, however. A tank and three men in Pink tuxedos paraded up and down her street, their eyes prowling into un-curtained windows—of which there weren't many, for the rumors of folk disappearing were quickly spreading. One of the men in pink was unusually tall, Eric noted. Even as Eric watched, the tank stopped before a Mexican boy in torn blue jeans and bundled in seven or so t-shirts to keep out the cold. Eric could hear them questioning the young child. The three men in pink finally surrounded him and threw him onto the tank, chaining him there. The tallest of them gave the boy a thwack when he yelped. His laugh sounded familiar, as if it might smell of cinnamon. The tank tore asphalt and drove away, the three men in pink hopping into a nearby car and following.

The first WeightAbate delivery arrived soon after. Eric had been waiting at Teresa's door for it.

While Teresa was happy to eat in, neither Eric nor Thomas could convince her to not attend the nightly anti-tank meetings, despite the abduction on her very street.

41. CENTURION, SCHMENTURION.

W e've reached the centurion mark, days ahead of schedule," one of the Pink Man's advisors announced. The Pink Man rubbed his hand along a nearby woman's butt and jerked his head toward the speaker. The woman caught his cue and asked, "What's a centurion?"

"What I meant was that we reached our goal of one hundred anti-tankers to be executed on Sacred Splinter Day. I was referring to Roman times. Centurions were officers in charge of one-hundred men."

"You mean it's been done before?" Pink Man blurted. When the assembled staff responded with silence, he continued, "We need a different number. Come up with one."

After much Googling, the number they came up with was 314.5. That number, everyone assured Pink Man, had never been publicly executed.

"How are we going to get the point five?"

One aide suggested a pregnant woman, but Pink Man ixnayed that idea. "My loving Christian supporters would never buy that half a person as just half a person. They have this idea about souls."

"What about a babe in swaddling?"

"This will occur at the manger celebration, remember?"

"What about a retard?"

"We need to be politically correct. And that correctness would also knock out any type of cripple or quadriplegic or deaf and dumb dummy."

Captain Carmel had been assigned guard duty that day. The captain was the leader of the squadron who'd executed four anti-tankers and retired to a Starbucks to drink mocha Grandes and munch almond protein bars while the fifth female anti-tanker supposedly lay bleeding and suffering by a wall. "Excuse me, gentlemen and ladies," the captain said, stepping forward to salute and click-clack his boot heels. "I have just the solution and know just the man to carry it out."

42. THE LOOP RETURNS.

Eric had suppressed 99.999 percent of the online clips featuring Teresa. One solitary clip of her eating that donut eluded him, however. He kept her as far away from social media as he could to avoid it and was feeling fairly confident. They attended nightly anti-tanker meetings. The membership continued to swell and Teresa enlisted Eric to help in simple one-column addition for dues. "Our membership is growing at an amazing rate," she commented. Hearing this, Eric bent down and lifted the bottom line upwards from the floor, and Teresa smiled, even without a glass of dry white wine.

Then, at one meeting, while Eric and Teresa chatted by the coffee, tea, and purified water stand, the same ultra-thin woman with the same blue shawl clacked her ultra-high blue high heels and strutted toward them.

"Well! Birds of a feather! As if double cream weren't bad enough, but you, our beloved treasurer, have to imbibe—inhale, I might better say—glazed donuts on the sly." The woman slung her blue shawl so that it brushed Teresa's face. "Or not so on the sly, since you're greedily munching one on the Internet where who knows how many innocents will see and be misled by your example. Happy wasteful munching!" The woman then slung her shawl at Eric. "Udder lover!" she hissed, walking off.

"What is she talking about?" Teresa began to shiver even as she asked this.

A nearby woman interceded. "Dear, we all have relapses. We all make mistakes." Then the woman's composure changed, "But Antoinette is right. Must you have allowed that glazed donut eating sequence to be filmed? And now, with it showing so prominent on the Internet! My two grandsons were clapping and yelping like heathen when they watched it. Propriety, propriety! And you, the esteemed treasurer of our Anti-Tankers Local 988!"

Teresa poured hot Ceylon tea on her left index finger and screamed, "I deserve that!"

Eric wished Precinct Eight employed a yapping recognition program so he might stalk this woman and the one with the slinging shawl.

43. THE LOOP MOBIUSES.

Anna the secretary stood to once more offer honey-and-oregano infused dog biscuits to PuckPooch, black coffee or Ceylon tea to Eric and Teresa. Eric violently waved his hand and shook his head to dissuade her as she jiggled the pot, since eight of Teresa's fingers were already bandaged with burns. PuckPooch howled in sympathy. Anna nodded wisely and led them in to the consultation room and its couch.

"Loops are ever so sneaky," Teresa the counselor intoned as Teresa sat and munched an oregano infused honey-baked dog biscuit, all that she deserved. "There are two ways to delete them, or they will Mobius back on you if you aren't careful. That's why we need to introduce the fifth dimension to them." She paused, "Or, more appropriately, introduce them to the fifth dimension."

"The fifth?" Eric asked. Teresa could not speak, for the oregano dog biscuit had swollen in her mouth, almost gagging her. *I deserve to gag*, she thought, wishing she could voice that confession aloud.

"Yes. The fifth dimension offers two paths. I derived both paths, both cures, from Kroger's pecan pies and what's-his-name, the boy I knew in high school. His path was the first way, the Way of Obliviscor. I fear though, that with *your* Loop and the public prevalence of your Loop's keyword, we must work within the Second Way, cloying. It's the Upper Path. It offers a more physical challenge."

Teresa the counselor crossed her legs. Eric and Teresa heard a hipbone pop. PuckPooch's ears straightened. Teresa the counselor grimaced and shifted in her hardback chair, placing it once more in the middle of the floor. A small marble-topped table sat next to her chair today.

"Yes. Indeed. So this morning, the four of us are going to cloy." She turned to face the door. "Anna! The Upper Path!" she called.

The secretary walked in with a stack of placards and what looked like a quart of cover-the-globe Sherwin-Williams paint. Instead of a globe for its logo, though, there was a brain. She placed the can and the placards on the small table. As she left the room, Eric noted that her high heels were blue and matched the shawl-slinging woman's. Teresa the counselor reached underneath her skinny bottom and produced a paintbrush. Had it made her hipbone pop so loudly?

"Will you be needing the smocks?" Anna asked, reopening the door and peeping back. A fearful lilt haunted her voice.

"That depends." Teresa looked at Teresa. "Are we going to be spelling it correctly, with eight letters, or the simplified form of five letters?"

Teresa had managed to swallow the oregano dog biscuit, so she answered. "I don't deserve simplified. Or maybe I do. Maybe that's all I deserve. Or maybe I don't."

"Oh my," Teresa the counselor replied. She turned to Anna. "Two smocks, for certain. I believe we're going to have to go whole hog and spell it both ways." She quickly turned to Teresa. "Please say you don't know French. Do you?"

"I only took a semester of Spanish in high school. I went to college in accounting."

"Praise Zeus for that. *Beignet, boules de Berlin...* those frogs and their pastries. They likely have ninety words for..." Teresa the counselor paused and studied Teresa's paling face. "Do you think you're ready to withstand the D word?"

Two on the couch leaned forward; one on the couch shrank back.

Teresa the counselor stood and donned the smock Anna handed her. She pulled a large knife from the waistband of her dress and clicked it. Eric's eyes widened. A switchblade? With it, she pried the small can open.

"Come here and don this smock, Teresa. Now, this is and this isn't paint. It's a raspberry-infused solution of raw honey, Napoleon brandy, and Clabber Girl baking powder. Clabber Girl's the only brand with enough oomph to make the mixture swell up and dry. With this not-paint paint, I'm going to paint not-paint letters—and you are going to guide my hand, Teresa—on these coconut-flavored placards, the cumulative letters forming that word you now so fear. Spelled both ways." She looked at Teresa, who still sat shrunken into the couch. "You know what that word is, don't you, Teresa."

Teresa nodded meekly.

"Good. Indeed. Come. Don your smock. Let us begin not-paint painting."

Teresa's hand was shaking so badly that it took thirty minutes to spell out the simplified version of *donut*. One letter per the five placards. She had to take a seat four times to stop shaking. The second, elongated version, *doughnut*, went a bit faster, taking only another thirty minutes, despite the added three letters and placards. And she only took a seat once.

"There, you see? Indeed, already the Cloying Principle and the Upper Path are taking effect. Once you eat these two words in their entirety, settle them in your belly, run them through your intestinal tract, reconstitute and emit them, your fears, your panic attacks, and your troubles will disappear." Teresa the counselor snapped her fingers. "Like that."

"Eat? Reconstitute?"

"But of course. That is the only Way on this Upper Path. And it must be a group effort. We will all chant the secret word 'Om' as we munch each letter. We will all four eat and reconstitute each letter, though you, Teresa, will have the—well, not the lion's, but let's call it the *canine's* share." Teresa the counselor gave a nod to PuckPooch, who was entranced by the ribbons dangling from the ceiling. *Movement*, his reptile brain thought. *Go for it*. Eric saw, too, and wondered if they could program dog-oids with primal emotions. Teresa the counselor continued, "You must eat just over half of each coconut flour placard. We three will eat the rest. Group therapy."

When Teresa and Teresa finished not-painting painting the thirteen letters on the thirteen coconut-flavored placards, Teresa the counselor insisted they wait while the raspberry gel dried. She shook off her smock and sat in the hardback chair. She moved back and breathed out forcefully through her mouth.

"Did you watch the Patriots-Bengals game?" she asked, letting her shoulders fall into simulated relaxation. "No? Well. Are you going to watch the Macy's Parade? I hear The Pink Man is going to pardon a special needs turkey."

44. ERUCTATION AT PRECINCT EIGHT.

Eric had made it to work early for the camaraderie coffee ever since the shaming he underwent his second day. Today, he burped as he opened the precinct's front door. He burped as he lifted his time card. He burped as he inserted it to be stamped. He burped as he drank camaraderie coffee with the other recruits and Lieutenant Riley. He burped as he powered up his station's computer and checked its diagnostics. With each burp, he tasted a raspberry-coconut mixture.

"That woman friend of yours is a fine specimen." It was Lieutenant Riley, who suddenly stood behind Eric. "Here, you and her might need this someday." Eric turned, and Lieutenant Riley handed him a small yellow card.

Get Out of Jail Free!

Eric looked at the card, felt its oily texture. He burped. Eric could almost see the raspberry-coconut molecules emitting to mix with Lieutenant Riley's cinnamon cologne and whatever odd oil resided on the card.

"That card's bona fide," Lieutenant Riley said, giving a sniff to the air. "As good as any governor's pardon. You know, that Teresa counselor woman, she helped me escape a Loop. I forget what she helped me forget, but that's why it worked, cause now I can go to the range any time, day or night, and shoot my Glock Zap Gun for several hundred rounds without flinching. Hell, several thousand if I wanted." As Lieutenant Riley mimicked his hands rising in endless recoils from a pistol, Eric burped. Lieutenant Riley pointed to the yellow card. "Stow that somewhere safe. You never know." With those words, the lieutenant walked away, wobbling as he did, raising his hands to reproduce more pistol recoils.

Was it Eric's imagination, or was the lieutenant taller this work shift?

45. SHOPPING AT KROGER'S.

Teresa insisted that they have a homemade Thanksgiving Day dinner, not a WeightAbate! meal.

"You know, my mother's mother's mother had a great recipe for oyster stuffing. I still have it. My dad's dad's dad always said that oysters will put lead in your pencil." Teresa paused and looked to PuckPooch. "What ever could that mean?"

Eric envisioned an old fashioned pencil. Weren't they long and turgid like the cigars Thomas gave them three times a week? Could it be that sometimes a pencil wasn't just a pencil? Eric smiled with insight. "Yes, yes, let's be sure to use that recipe," he said. "It sounds… levitating."

"Levitating?" Teresa asked.

"You know, elongating."

"Elongating?"

"You know what I mean. Uplifting. Words. Who can beat 'em?"

Since they had known one another, Eric and Teresa had kissed nineteen and-a-half times. A half because Teresa once had angrily turned her head away at the last moment to glare at a Support Your Local Tanks poster. They had held hands forty-four times. Eric had massaged out her charley horses thirty-nine times. One evening Teresa had commented upon an "odd tingling sensation" as he massaged her thigh. But they had never consummated. Perhaps, just perhaps, an aphrodisiac like oysters was called for.

They went to shop at the nearest Kroger's. Eric was breathing heavily as he walked briskly through the parking lot and into the entrance. The electronic doors opened widely and happily, giving a gushy, squishy, warmly cushioning welcome. Eric stiffened. Sometimes, he thought, a door's not just a door. He looked back to see Teresa practicing her look right, look left, look right again, look left again precaution. But there were no posters in the parking lot. Was she just keeping in tone? When Teresa at last entered, he gave her a tiny smooch on the cheek by the carts.

In his excitement at her smile, Eric filled the shopping cart half full within six minutes of entering the store. At the produce aisle, he lifted a bunch of purple grapes. "Grapes to tempt the Greek gods and goddesses. Aphrodite, Venus, Dionysius, Apollo." Then, taking two steps, he lifted a bag of apples. "Apples for Adam and Eve and their pet snake." The bananas sent him into ecstasy. He balanced a bunch on his head. He cradled two bunches at his bosom. He wobbled even larger bunches before his crotch.

"Fruit has plenty of roughage and vitamin C," Teresa commented. "That's a good bottom line." She bent to place the back of her hand on the floor and gave off a second smile.

"That's right, that's right," Eric encouraged. His eyes lit as they neared the peppers. Bright Christmas green jalapenos. Thick-skinned poblanos. Lengthy thick Cubanelles, which he placed beside the bananas, wiggling them to Teresa's amusement. Deep shiny orange and *caliente* habaneros.

In the dairy aisle, Eric plopped the spunkiest cheeses into their cart. Camembert, Jarlsberg Swiss, bleu, and Roquefort. Tubs of Greek yogurt with all those living, procreative cultures and more fruit came next. Hidden blueberries that would give off a pleasant pop in their mouths. Butter. Sticks of it that he imagined melting down and oozing into a charley-horse curing lotion.

At the meat counter, they encountered… surely it was Lieutenant Riley. He appeared much shorter today, though the cinnamon cologne wafted precipitously. He was holding up a package of turkey drumsticks, which he waved in the cool Kroger air. "There's not a thing better for a young couple to eat. Face-to-face, weaving them in the air like basted batons, slowly and deliberately gnawing them down to the gristle, placing the stripped and elongated bones crisscross on their plates, eyeing one another after a glass of dry white wine and a double helping of oyster dressing. Bumping knees. Grooming one another. Licking each other's elongated fingers. Running their tongue tips perilously along the other's fingernails. A jar of warm honey or a tub of room temperature Cool Whip lying in wait on the table between them. Why not both? And some dark chocolate syrup, too."

Eric leaned forward, ready to query the man speaking. "Lieutenant Riley?" Instead of responding, the short man simply dropped the package of drumsticks into their cart and walked off. Surely, it was the lieutenant, though his head didn't even come to the third shelf of Cheese-Its and Doritos he passed, despite the pomade in his yellow hair.

46. THE VITALITY DANCE HOLOGRAPH.

Wednesday. Thanksgiving Day tomorrow!

Teresa and Eric went to the anti-tanker meeting. The shawl-slinging woman strode straight for them. "Donut dunker!" she shouted. Teresa only smiled and continued bobbing her Ceylon tea bag in a cup's nearly boiling water. Her fingers had healed thanks to a miracle salve Anna the secretary recommended. "We keep it for cutters," she confided. "I used to be one before I took the First Path. The second, Upper Path is scary. You're so brave to take it," she'd said.

Now, looking straight at the shawl-slinger and using a waiter's showy up-and-down motion, Eric poured triple, quadruple cream into his coffee, turning it beyond tan into chalky. He then slurped the result and offered the woman a taste. She stumbled backwards. She turned. She fled.

The purpose of the night's meeting was to plan a meeting date for planning their activity for the Sacred Splinter Day. But since there were so many days still available before that day and so many conflicting obligations, they adjourned early, agreeing to put off that plan for the next meeting. Planning a planning meeting date was evidently going to take some planning, Eric thought. Maybe they should plan a date to plan the date to plan the date.

One thing the meeting did accomplish however, was the distribution of a brand spanking new holograph Vitality Dance program, which was viewed as both an innovative recruiting tool and as a home-use spiritual self-improvement aid. Teresa was especially excited, so excited that she memorized the fifteen-digit code for downloading the program and sent it electronically ahead to Eric's apartment so the holograph would begin playing the moment they entered.

"Won't that scare PuckPooch?" Eric wondered.

"Oh no," Teresa replied. "I've been talking to PuckPooch. I can affirm that he's ready to become an anti-tanker." She paused, rubbing her knuckles against Eric's in what might have been the secret handshake, though he wasn't certain. "Unlike some holdout people I know," Teresa added.

The air hung balmy, nearly warm. They were standing beside the meeting hall and Eric studied the sky. He almost saw a star, he thought, through the smog. *Venus? Of course, that's not a star*, he chided himself. A star that was a star that wasn't a star. Still and all, it was the star of Love, no matter. Eric sighed.

Eric was in love, all right, but he fearlessly maintained his anti-everything stance. All matters considered, doing so seemed wise and healthy. He *was*, after all, employed at the Precinct Eight Police Department. Teresa's brother, after all, *was* a lawyer in the system. And Teresa *was* a member of the anti-tanker movement, even though she'd never assaulted a tank. And then, whenever Eric thought of Willy Taylor's wife . . . well what good did joining a movement and getting her Pink Man Card sent by registered mail do for her? No, anti-everything seemed the smartest route. More than that, it seemed the truest route. Whatever truth could mean these days.

A block away from his apartment, they heard PuckPooch yipping and barking.

"It's a happy bark," Teresa insisted. "The Vitality Dance holograph has started just on time."

The two sped up their walk, and sure enough when they opened the door, they saw PuckPooch hopping and playfully nipping at the holograph dancers. Eric laughed. But then he noted that one of the dancers was the shawl-tossing woman. How had she wriggled her way in? Some purity test? A twenty-page dietary exam? Eric watched her long tanning-spa legs flash upward. Was she hoping for an audition in Hollywood? Radio City? And then Eric couldn't believe it: a

Lieutenant Riley, restored to his majestic height, was kicking up his legs alongside the shawl-tosser. It had to be the lieutenant, though his hair was thick and dark, like a reincarnated Elvis. A wig, of course. Or was the lieutenant's yellow hair a wig? Just where did truth lie? *Lying Truth*. Eric smiled at that thought, an oxymoron, if ever. From what little he'd seen of Precinct Eight's operations, Truth always lay about lying.

He looked from the holograph to see that Teresa had already joined in, waving a celery stick from the WeightAbate! program in the air as she kicked her legs higher and higher. Hoping for a charley horse, Eric walked into the kitchen and opened the refrigerator to eye the two turkey legs. He ran his hand over the package the lieutenant had dropped in their cart. Whether yellow or charcoal black, the hair atop the lieutenant's head had sprouted a fine idea for Thanksgiving dinner tomorrow. From the living room, he could hear Teresa's grunts as she kicked higher and higher. Any moment now, any moment now... once again, she hadn't warmed up with stretches. Eric took out a stick of butter and put it in the microwave.

47. A THANKSGIVING MORAL.

The Macy's Thanksgiving Day parade was usually 2.65 miles long. This year it was taking two extra jogs, which would make it 2.9 miles long. This came about when The Pink Man announced he would perform two special patriotic services in the parade. The first was the pardoning of the Special Needs Turkey. The second was to be a surprise. The surprise was actually a test run for the Splinter Day execution of 314-and-a-half bad people. It was Captain Carmel who had suggested this simple Thanksgiving Day trial.

The first patriotic service came early, when the parade detoured into a pristine courtyard where The Pink Man himself stood waiting, petting what was labeled a special needs turkey. The Green Life First Party claimed this turkey was autistic, born that way from the gene modification grain its dame had imbibed. Alas, this young tom turkey could not gobble. The Green Life First Party bemoaned the fact that it would never be fulfilled in its lifetime, that it was thwarted by corporate greed and scientific abuse, that its spirit would roam forever searching out just one fulfilling and soulful gobble, just one glorious moment of loving communication with its fellow species-mates. This, the Green Life First Party wailed, is "WHAT HAPPENS WHEN!"

The Pink Man had been allotted ten minutes to speak and pet the turkey, tug its wattle, console its soulessness. But then—Lo!—the turkey let out a gobble halfway through The Pink Man's speech. The Pink Man turned and declared it miraculously cured, giving his infamous crooked-tooth grin. "He's undergone fulfillment, he's ready for the drumstick oven." Twenty schoolchildren nearby began to wail and cry. The Pink Man nodded, and an aide snapped their collective photo. As the childish blubbering increased, The Pink Man relented and spent fifteen minutes explaining that he was just kidding. "Terrific Tom the Turkey will lead a life of vocational luxury in our household," The Pink Man assured the children.

So the parade lagged ten minutes behind schedule, and would soon lag even more, for The Pink Man hopped into a PinkMobile, accompanied by a young female aide carrying the now sedated turkey. The PinkMobile led the parade, taking time to stop whenever any attractive woman in a short skirt—despite the late November chill that had set in just that pre-dawn morning—jumped and waved and shouted on a street corner. Watching the TV, Eric saw one blonde do so. It was like she was performing a Vitality Dance for Singles, he thought. He buried that thought deep in a back pocket, however, seeing Teresa's frown as she, too, watched the hopping woman. The Pink Man tossed a ten-ounce pack of pink cherry-flavored gummie bears at the cavorting woman. He'd already done this six times in the parade.

"Disgusting," Teresa commented. "I wouldn't be surprised if he slipped his cell number and a prophylactic inside the package."

"I've heard The Pink Man doesn't believe in rubbers," Eric commented. "He wants to be a natural man."

Teresa was right. Eric was wrong. The Pink Man did inscribe his private cell number on each packet. But while The Pink Man also did deeply desire to rub his foreskin *mano a womano*, so to speak, and though he also did deeply desire to father as many little Pink Men as possible, he also did harbor an abnormal fear of social diseases. As well he should, the young female aide thought as she tried to calm the reviving turkey with more food pellets infused with a tranquilizer while at the same time tugging her bra where The Pink Man had grabbed it to give a playful, mannish snap.

Teresa and Eric were watching the parade from Eric's apartment. Ever since another YouTube episode of the dubious clip showing Teresa standing amid tank carnage while anti-tankers kicked corpses and hiked their legs had emerged on the Internet, Eric and Thomas insisted she avoid her apartment. Especially since yet one more child, a teenage girl of suspicious racial origin, had been summarily arrested on her street.

"Safety first," Thomas had insisted.

"Look left, look right; then look left and right again," Eric added.

It was Eric's admonition that convinced her.

"So many various corporations sponsored Pink Man floats," the TV announcer was giddily proclaiming, "that there are well over two dozen in the parade."

"He's so beloved," his co-host said with a sigh. "It's been rumored that one of the popes was going to attend," the cohost continued.

"But that's proven untrue," the announcer countered, inserting a tinge of sadness to his giddiness. "His Holiness One had previously committed to a speech in Paris, and His Holiness Two was called to baptize the corpses of fifty refugee children within twenty-four hours of their deaths to assure they'd not be confined to Limbo."

"So caring," his cohost inserted. Then, both announcers stated that there was going to be a special "moral spectacle" at precisely halfway through the parade.

The word *moral* stopped Eric stop mid-sip in his coffee. He let go of Teresa's hand. He stood and began to pace, accidentally stepping on PuckPooch's tail.

A moral, a moral, a moral. It's about time, Eric thought.

At exactly one-point-four-five miles, the parade did halt. The Pink Man emerged from the PinkMobile, leaving the female aide shoving yet one more tranquilizer pellet down the tom turkey's gullet while straightening her re-tangled bra. She worried that a strap might be broken.

As The Pink Man exercised his jowls and pressed his hand against his lapel, the newly formed Space Corps Band started playing "Home on the Range," a song research had shown could lower the systolic blood pressure of farmers in the country's wheat belt by as much as fourteen points. The Pink Man saluted the band.

Eric leaned forward, curious, hopeful, as to the upcoming moral. Teresa too, leaned, though something tingled in her stomach. It was an unhappy tingle. It resembled, in fact, more of a twitch than a tingle, more of a spasm than a twitch. It resembled, in fact, the same pain the off-mark marksman in the firing squad had undergone. She longed to start the Vitality Dance holograph and shut off the TV, forget the Macy's Parade. Something, however, left her immobile while at the same time tugging her forward. Was it zeitgeist? Spirit time?

The Space Corps Band quieted. The Pink Man looked to the sky as if it were his true audience. Maybe it is, Eric thought. Teresa, in a moment of solid naiveté, thought that maybe The Pink Man had viewed a Vitality Dance holograph before breakfast and was somehow undergoing momentous spiritual growth.

"Thanks. Giving. Day. Family. Patriotism. Greatness." The Pink Man here paused, though he was still staring at the blue sky. "Goodness," he added, as if the sky had provided another precious word.

Now he looked into the cameras. "But there is bad stuff too. Very bad stuff and very bad people and very bad families. Yes, I said that: 'bad families.'" The Pink Man gave a crooked-tooth, of-the-people smile. Dentists nationwide clapped. "Like bad apples, bad families must be weeded from the compost pile. The sun can't shine in the shade, you know." The Pink Man paused, and the female co-host cooed while the announcer whispered, "That's so true."

The Pink Man saluted the Space Corps Band again, and an officer in a bright pink Space Corps uniform stepped forward, a newly manufactured laser rifle at port arms. The Pink Man saluted him back. The officer did an about-face and walked briskly to a wall where four people were tied to posts.

"That's Willy!" Eric shouted.

Teresa's stomach was actually roiling now. She swayed and gagged.

"Willy Taylor! Tied to that post! You met him! He recommended that counselor for us! He got me my first job!"

The two of them watched as the Space Corps officer handed a sheet of pink paper to The Pink Man. Giving the paper a crisp shake, The Pink Man intoned, "Whereas, the Taylor family has most willfully and most violently derelicted its duties to the nation and to global morality in general; whereas, the grand dame of the Taylor family was found guilty of anti-tank sentiments four years ago and executed; whereas the remaining husband and three progeny did not reconcile with global morality and this grandly great nation, but rather further and willfully subverted happiness and family values into vile treason, I hereby pronounce the Taylor Family to be bad oats. Very, very bad oats." The Pink Man turned to the officer. It was Captain Carmel who snapped to attention. "Captain, do your duty."

A firing squad of five emerged from a portico with the newly manufactured laser rifles.

"Present arms!" Captain Carmel shouted. "Ready!" The Pink Man shrugged his shoulders manfully and jutted his lower jaw even more manfully. "Aim!" The captain gave a wink to the man closest to him in the firing squad. "Fire!"

Instead of resounding cracks, five sizzles buzzed through the air. Three bodies slumped immediately, the fourth writhed against the post.

The Pink Man nodded and a barista wheeled a cart up to serve the firing squad and its captain Almond Latte Grandes and coconut protein bars. In the background, one body continued to writhe. Captain Carmel winked at the nearest man and turned to receive The Pink Man's grandest crooked tooth smile. This practice run to show that Captain Carmel could efficiently deliver on his promise of a half for the Sacred Splinter Day event was an outstanding success. The Pink Man saluted him and entered the PinkMobile. The Tom was not seen. The aide had fed him sufficient pellets that it lay passed out behind a seat.

"Willy was African American," Teresa said, peering into the TV closely enough to form cataracts or skin cancer. "And his son was as tall as him."

Eric sat stunned. "He is. He was. He is."

"Two of those kids were Mexican. I think that small one was the kid they'd picked up on my street last week. Maybe the other one was too. She was tall. And the other was…"

Eric looked. Teresa was right. The young boy was short, his skin was brown, and he couldn't have even been in middle school. And the tall girl's skin was brown too. The other girl looked Chinese. Eric got close to the television and looked at the writhing man. It was Willy all right. That much was true. Eric was afraid to even think the word *Moral*. He vaguely imagined eating five coconut placards with each letter of that word painted with not-paint.

48. THANKSGIVING DAY SUBLIMITY.

We can't sit like this forever," Teresa said. It was noon. The Space Corps Band had just finished *Hail to the Chief!* The two announcers were cooing like dirty city pigeons eying cat offal. "Why not?" Eric countered with a mumble.

One o'clock came. They sat side-by-side, not touching, and stared at a taco commercial on the TV. If only Eric and Teresa had been facing one another, they could have been re-enacting *My Brother, My Sister.* But then, they would have had to have been speaking, also.

"We can't—" Teresa didn't finish her sentence, but just stared at the screen where a huge black truck rumbled over huge rocks while two girls sat in its bed laughing and eating a salad. "So safe and smooth, you could serve a five course dinner," the commercial proclaimed.

Two o'clock came. Eric thought he had to pee but ignored the tingle. Teresa felt a cramp in her leg but ignored the tingle. On TV, a man was playing piano and a woman was singing beside him while a fire roared around them and a chandelier fell. "With our insurance, nothing will bother you," the commercial proclaimed.

Three o'clock came. "Teresa," Eric said.

"Eric," Teresa replied.

For some reason, the TV had shut itself off. The two of them continued to stare as if nothing had changed. Eric hadn't even noticed that Teresa used his real name. Neither had Teresa.

At four p.m. Maslow took over. Eric went to pee, washed his hands, and placed the two drumsticks in the oven. Teresa dolloped oysters into the dressing. As she did, Eric lightly massaged her thigh.

They both gave out sighs.

At six p.m. they sat to eat.

The browned drumsticks stuck in the air like the dead Mexican boy's legs as the laser bolt hit him, and his legs spasmed upward.

The two sweet potatoes lay as deflated as Willy's other two not-children children had as they slumped against the post.

The salad shown as green as the AstroTurf lawn where the execution had been conducted.

The green peas glared at them like dying eyeballs.

The cranberries looked as red as the blood that didn't spill from the Laser bolts.

The bottle of dry white wine stood as unopened and still as Eric and Teresa.

PuckPooch blinked. It was the first blink since the parade had finished.

49. BACK TO WORK—NOT.

On Friday, Eric called in sick to the Precinct Eight Police station. Lieutenant Riley answered the phone and offered to bring some chicken soup by that evening.

Teresa called next and informed the Anti-tankers that she wouldn't be able to collect or enter new dues that night. Antoinette replied, "Have a hot date at Darryl's Delectable Donut Depot?"

All day, PuckPooch lay atop their feet, keeping them warm.

50. WHAT THE FOURTH ESTATE THOUGHT.

The gentlefolk of the fourth estate, those journalists who protect and guarantee freedom, promulgated the following about the Patriotic Thanksgiving Day Bad Oats Moral.

Scientific American: "Fifty years ago—and geology shows us how short that timespan is—executions were a sloppy affair. Blood and flesh spattered with the use of bullets; torturous screams and shattered teeth in the case of electricity; retching and convulsions in the case of delivered toxins. Now, with the advent of the first GE laser rifles, a neat, efficient, nearly circular .57 centimeter hole delivers. Technology provides."

Mother Earth News: "Of the two 'morals' delivered to us on Thanksgiving Day at the Macy's Parade, surely the most lasting is the so-called miraculous cure of Tom Turkey. What is labeled 'miraculous' by those in power is more truly nature bounding forth, despite callous genetic manipulations, despite non-organic feeds, despite this planet's undue warming. But nature cannot battle alone. We must help her. We must stand tall and each perform out best to maintain, maintain, maintain."

Harper's: "T. S. Eliot wrote of his magus, *'Were we led all that way for birth or death? There was a birth, certainly . . . and a death, our death.'* Our nation, indeed our world, certainly seems in turmoil as we every day face birth and death. Are the births to be capitalized as Births? Are the deaths to be capitalized as Deaths? Those are questions we must ponder.

The New Yorker [N. B. This issue was affected by a Lunker's Union Strike, which when combined with derailment of a train carrying paper for the magazine's printing, delayed the issue until Christmas Eve. In conjunction, The New Yorker's *electronic server was hacked, delaying the dissemination of this article on the Internet until that same December date.]* "Again, The Pink Man has delivered. Just what he has delivered is to be debated, however. His supporters no doubt saw Truth and Justice stomping forward with the execution of the Taylor Family. Others will beg to differ. Others will see the whimpers and crawling of a self-aggrandizing tyrant."

Washington Post: "Our leader has performed an amazing feat! Within a brief half-hour he has shown his empathy, his ability to think on his feet, and his compassion—all countered with a stern appraisal of danger and a swift elimination of said danger. The double pardon of Tom Turkey and the swift condemnation of the Taylors—whose name is now synonymous with infamy and Benedict Arnold—will long stand in our history."

L. A. Times: "When will the East Coast understand? My wife, our two children, and I were regaled with eating our eggs benedict and drinking our o.j. by a comatose and then gobbling turkey and then the execution of four would-be traitors. There is a time zone! Please respect it and act accordingly."

Tuscaloosa News: "Crimson Tide Nets Another Five-star Recruit!"

51. AN ENCOUNTER OUTSIDE THE LOOP.

On Saturday a week later, Eric, Teresa, and PuckPooch walked to Darryl's Delectable Donut Depot. Even though Darryl no longer served donuts because of the ongoing sugar moratorium, he made the best fluffy biscuits ("So light they float!"), served with the smoothest raw honey in the city. Or with non-sulfured molasses or patty sausage if you wanted. Or Stevia, if you wanted, for Darryl did not share Teresa the Counselor's qualms about mixing the latter in hot liquids. Eric himself held a warm spot for Darryl ever since that Labor Day five years back when Darryl had saved him from the tanks. And too, going to Darryl's provided something of a small test. It continually amazed Eric how cleanly Teresa the counselor's reclamation program had worked on Teresa, for she never flinched at Darryl's huge neon sign pronouncing D-O-N-U-T-S!   D-O-N-U-T-S!   D-O-N-U-T-S!

Workers would soon, of course, be changing the sign to read, B-I-S-C-U-I-T-S!   B-I-S-C-U-I-T-S!   B-I-S-C-U-I-T-S!

"That kid looks familiar," Eric said when they neared the shop. A lanky Black teenager stood before the display window, counting the change in his hand. PuckPooch wagged his tail, but then PuckPooch wagged his tail at any stranger. PuckPooch especially wagged his tail at young humans, and this Black boy was surely not quite out of high school.

"It's Billy Taylor!" Eric looked to Teresa, grabbing her arm. "Willy Taylor's son!"

"That poor orphan child," Teresa replied, tilting her head at Eric's hand on her arm.

Billy Taylor looked up from counting his money. He gave Eric and PuckPooch a grand smile. "Hello, Mr. Eric. I got your old job. Aw man, I wish I had my tennis ball, PuckPooch. They won't let me take it to work, and I just got off."

"We're so sorry about your dad," Teresa said.

Since Thanksgiving, she'd graduated from tanks, tanks, tanks, to a more human form of communication. Her brother Thomas attributed this to the dry white wine; Eric thought maybe it was a combination of PuckPooch and the Patriotic Thanksgiving Day Bad Oats Cleansing. And, sure, dry white wine.

"He was nice, if I remember right," Billy replied, giving Teresa a faint smile, then turning back to counting his money. "That job you had sure don't pay much, does it, Mr. Eric?"

"Come on, our treat," Eric said. "We'll just go in to get some biscuits and honey for us all, though PuckPooch likes his best with patty sausage."

"My sister, if I remember right, she liked to eat them that way, too. She was pretty nice, if I remember right. But I try not to remember too much. I don't want to get stuck in no Loop."

PuckPooch gave a whine.

"That a dog-oid? I forget."

"We don't know," Eric said.

"No, of course he's not," Teresa insisted.

"That's good," Billy said. "I think that my big brother wanted to get a dog. But then he and my sister left, and I didn't see them no more. I wish I'd known my mother more, maybe. She was nice. I think my dad always said she was, anyway. Them biscuits in that window sure look good, don't they?"

52. TERESA'S LAST CHARLEY HORSE?

For some reason, Teresa was upset when Eric got home from the police station on Monday. Instead of entering the growing dues and contributions as the bottom line on the Anti-tanker books, she had switched on the Vitality Dance holograph. With a glance from the front door, Eric thought that she'd revved it up two or three times the normal speed, though he wasn't sure this was possible.

"What's wrong?" he asked.

"Wrong? Wrong?" she replied, kicking each leg higher as if wanting to clip the ceiling fan in his apartment.

Eric looked to the holograph to see Antoinette twirling her blue wrap and swirling sensually about the man who so resembled Lieutenant Riley. Eric's right leg twitched, for the Vitality Dance was quite catchy, after all. It had a beat.

"I mean, isn't this early in the afternoon to be..." Eric's voice faded, for Teresa was leaping wildly among the holograph's dancers, outdoing them all. Eric thought about joining, just to see if he could catch where and when the extra dancer would drop out. The holograph was a true minyan in this sense. There were always ten and only ten dancers. It was downright spooky at times. How could a holograph know?

Teresa usually encouraged Eric to join her. And always, always, always, a dancer would drop out. This afternoon, though, she was wrapped up in the dance, herky-jerky to the Nth degree. Her chest heaved. Her legs flung wildly. It was almost as if she were angrily kicking Antoinette's ghostly 3-D image, though of course that was impossible, for the Vitality Dance promoted such spiritual ease that all anger, all worry, all fear dissipated as easily as that extra minyan dancer dropped from the lineup.

Teresa's kicks turned so extravagant that Eric slipped into the kitchen for two sticks of butter and put them into a bowl and then into the microwave.

"Wrong? Wrong? Nothing's wrong!" Teresa shouted from the living room. Almost as magically as the continual minyan, the microwave's ding coincided with Teresa's scream. Another charley horse.

Eric ran into the living room and shut down the holograph. Teresa lay on the floor holding her right leg.

"Wrong? Wrong? Nothing's wrong," she kept shouting, even as Eric rubbed butter into her calf.

And when he carried her to bed, her shouts turned to sobs, "Wrong? Wrong? Nothing's wrong." Occasionally, during the night, Eric would feel her turn to whimper, "Wrong? Wrong? Nothing's wrong."

53. THE NUMBER ACHIEVED.

The very day after Teresa's last charley horse she insisted that she needed to go back to her apartment and retrieve a picture of her mother. Eric almost blurted that he didn't know she had a mother, though of course that was silly, unless she were an android. And except for dog-oids and cat-oids, those new creatures were in an awkward stage of development and could speak only in a clipped fashion with limited answers, and they made no true eye contact. Anti-tankers joked they were like The Pink Man's advisors. Pink Man supporters joked they were like anti-tankers. So Eric just nodded in agreement to Teresa. PuckPooch sidled up to him and moaned lowly.

"Our mother was a combat nurse in the Great Mexican Wall War," Thomas told Eric on Skype. "I think that's where she met our father, though I forget."

Do you remember if he was a nice guy, Eric almost asked. Then he thought about his own father and mother. How long since he'd thought of them? All he remembered of them were that they were nice, and Teresa the counselor hadn't even worked her magic to fade his memory. It seemed to forget on its own.

"Oh, I didn't know that," was all that Eric managed to say over the phone to Thomas.

So Thomas and Eric insisted Teresa wait, insisted they should accompany her to her apartment. And when they did early next morning, they encountered a tank at the end of her block and half a dozen or more pinkly clad soldiers wandering about, peeping in windows along the street. From the driver's seat, Thomas waved to one, who waved and smiled back.

"I got him off a manslaughter charge," Thomas whispered to Eric, while still waving. Teresa sat in the back seat, hugging PuckPooch.

Eric thought he saw Lieutenant Riley sitting on that same park bench, munching another breakfast. That tall man, whoever it was, waved back also, dropping a crumb to a waiting pigeon and not even kicking it away. It seemed to be a friendly street in the pink morning sun. But the tanks belied that friendliness.

"It's in my bedroom," Teresa said at the front door while energetically wiping her feet on the *I Heart Tanks* doormat. Eric looked down to see that the black electrician's tape was still in place.

Thomas stood guard at the front door. Eric checked through the apartment, warning Thomas to keep an eye on the tall guy on the bench. Teresa said the photograph was in her bedroom, that she knew exactly where it was, that she'd just be a minute. Eric went to the apartment's back door. He peeked through the window to see a man who looked like Lieutenant Riley eating an apple. The man waved. Wasn't it the same guy Thomas claimed he'd gotten off a manslaughter charge?

A minute passed.

Three minutes passed.

Five.

"Teresa?" Thomas and Eric called in unison.

There came no answer. They called again. No answer. They ran into her bedroom to find the street-level window open. A pink note was taped to it.

Sic semper anti-tankers!

54. A REMINDER.

When Eric and Thomas rushed into the street from Teresa's apartment, they saw both tanks twisting about to leave, ripping more asphalt as they did. They ran after them, but the tanks were too fast. Eric turned and ran back to the bench. It was empty, save some McDonald's wrappers. There was also an unused straw still in its wrapper.

"Hey, mister," a Mexican kid said, giving Eric's shirt a tug.

Eric turned, and the kid said, "A stinky tall man gave me five Pinkers to come up to you and say, 'Don't forget the card I gave you.' He said you'd give me five more."

Eric didn't have any Pinkers on him, but Thomas did, and he gave five to the kid, who ran off, declaring he was going to buy beer.

They found the photograph on the floor in Teresa's bedroom. Thomas blinked twice as he held it before him. Eric watched him mouth the word "Mom." Taking it, they closed Teresa's apartment and headed for the city jail.

55. TERESA ARRESTED.

Teresa had paused when she picked up her mother's photograph. In it, her mother wore a uniform, for indeed she had been a nurse in what she called The Great Walrus War. She called it that because neither side wanted to fight. "We'd exchange cheeseburgers and tamales and fried chicken wings every mid-morning, tell racist jokes about mud-skin, cotton-skin, coal-skin," her mother had often told Teresa. "The trick was, you had to tell a joke about your own skin color. But, of course, people still got shot. People'd get sick and blame it on the cheeseburgers or tacos or fried chicken wings or the hot sauce or the mayonnaise or fried chili peppers. That war kept me busy enough."

As Teresa reminisced about her mother, three men in pink emerged from her closet and knocked her mother's photograph from her hand. Part of Teresa thought she deserved to be grabbed and have her mouth covered and her arm twisted. And then part of her thought she deserved to be pushed through a window and onto the street.

Another part of her thought, *You damned pink-o tanker bastards!* And she kicked the man nearest her as if she were in the finalist contest for the latest version of the Vitality Dance. When the man went down with a yelp, his two partners just laughed. "Kick all you want, sister! Your kicking days will soon be over. You're lucky number 314."

Part of Teresa wondered what that could possibly mean. Part of her knew exactly what it meant. Part of Teresa wondered where her brother Terry was. Another part of her wondered where her brother Thomas was. Part of her remembered a soft buttery massage as she was shoved into a lorry, and her leg cramped from the kick she delivered to another man in pink.

Who had massaged me so gently before? part of her wondered.

Ah, Harold, part of her remembered. *Ah, Errol,* part of her remembered. *Ah, Eric,* part of her remembered.

And then, as the lorry door shut, all of her despaired.

56. GET OUT OF JAIL FREE!

Thomas cancelled his court appearance. Eric called in sick.

Together they inspected the yellow card from Eric's wallet.

Get out of jail free!

"Lieutenant Riley gave it to me," Eric explained to Thomas.

"*The* Lieutenant Riley? A short guy with a walrus moustache?"

"He's tall and clean-shaven," Eric replied.

"That's him. A master of disguise. I got him off a triple Murder-One charge."

Ah, Eric thought, *no flimsy manslaughter charge for the Lieutenant.*

When they arrived at the Precinct Eight jail, they found it surrounded by tanks.

"We're celebrating," a tank commander returning from the precinct's bathroom told them, snapping both thumbs over his head and giving a tiny kick. "We just took in number 314. The half that's still out there is going to be sorted by God." He winked and climbed onto the tank, giving out another kick and a "Yahoo!"

Eric and Thomas looked at one another, not comprehending, but yet comprehending, somewhere, say in their right big toe or their left elbow or a fatty-tissue earlobe.

Inside the jail's entrance, Thomas stopped at a desk and said he was a lawyer and wanted to see the woman just brought it. The policeman jutted his jaw in imitation of The Pink Man and handed Thomas a number.

11,412.5

"Busy today. You got you a pretty long wait," the policeman said.

"Here now," Eric insisted. "Look here!" And he waved the *Get out of Jail Free!* card.

"Why didn't you just say so?" the policeman asked. He stood and snatched the number back from Thomas, saying, "Gotta do every little bit we can to help the environment." He placed the number neatly on a pile and then pointed them toward a side door with a single small window. The door was made from some dark wood, maybe cherry. Eric looked about: everything in the large room seemed to be either darkly tinted wood or stainless steel. People milled about, unwrapping candy bars and eating them. A child picked up a wrapper on the floor and poured a single orange M&M into her hand, then ate it. The child's mother slapped the packet from her hand back onto the floor. Three men watching jostled one another and laughed. A teenage girl busily texted on her cell phone. A teenage boy stood four feet away doing the same. They shyly looked at one another, giggled, and waved. A policeman sat on a stainless steel stool beside the dark wood door, playing with his cell phone. He raised a warning finger as Eric and Thomas approached. That finger quickly went back to popping numbers or figures on the cell phone.

Eric leaned. The man was playing *Anti-tankers, Tanks, Blips and Blanks.*

They waited for five minutes until the policeman twisted his torso, cursed, and shook the cell phone angrily, feigning to toss it on the wood floor. He then looked up. "Help you?"

Thomas's face was glowing with anger. Eric put his hand on Thomas's arm to silence him. Eric held up the *Get Out of Jail Free!* card. The policeman grunted and reached under his crotch to pull out a pink electronic pad. He sniffed the pad twice, shook it, and sniffed it again, his nose wriggling in pleasure. Satisfied, he punched in four numbers and stuck it back under his crotch. The cherry door beside him clicked, opening backward half an inch as if weighted. As they pushed it open and walked in, Eric looked to see the policeman once more on his cell phone, twisting his body as if putting a mojo on the game.

Twenty feet away, over another floor littered with candy wrappers, a policewoman stood at serious, erect attention before another door. This door was really pig-wire set into concrete. The pig-wire was locked with a huge Master Lock the size of Eric's head. The woman was inordinately tall, and Eric at first thought she might be the captain, whom he'd not seen since orientation day. But this woman was a redhead. Besides, why would a captain be guarding a jail door made of pig-wire?

But it was the Captain.

"Captain, ma'am!" Eric saluted.

She nodded curtly at them both and took the card from Eric. She twisted it in the fluorescent lighting and then put it between her right canine teeth and bit down three times. "Okay, you can pass through." She reached into her bra and pulled out an ovoid pink machine, and punched numbers on it. Eric noted that her left breast was now deflated. A key slid out from the wall behind her.

"Wait!" the captain shouted. "I need to do a retina scan on you both."

She led them to the wall and had them stand, each in turn, upon the outline of two shoes and stare directly at the wall, which opened suddenly and sent a great flash. Even though Eric went second, he still was not prepared for the intensity of the flash. He and Thomas stumbled through the pig-wire to round a corridor, where his vision cleared.

This corridor was marked with yard lines, like a football field. They walked ten yards, and a pink flag popped from the wall. Ten more, another flag. Then another. They turned a corner. Another flag, another ten yards. At the halfway mark, the fifty-yard line, canned cheers started, emitting from the ceiling. When they finished one hundred yards, the roar of the recorded crowd became deafening. An android with patchy pink skin popped out from a guard booth, wobbling to balance itself.

"Identification, please, ma'am."

Eric and Thomas looked at one another and shrugged. They each handed over the requisite Metro, County, State, and National identification cards.

"One moment, sirs." The android stepped backward, nearly tripping over a strip of aluminum in the floor.

Two minutes later, the android emerged, handing them their four ID cards plus two pink facemasks.

"Please wear these for the duration of your visit. There has been an outbreak of...." The android's mouth worked on itself. "An outbreak of... Thank you, ma'ams, for your cooperation."

A door opened beside the android, and Eric and Thomas entered after donning the masks.

Fluorescent lighting came on at their first movement. A water fountain was now spaced every ten yards. The first fountain had a sign, *Out of Order*. All nine remaining fountains had the same sign, though each intermittently shook as if its refrigeration unit was trying to start but failed because of moral turpitude. Moisture accumulating in Eric's mask became sticky.

Another door loomed before them. There was no one before it, and it slid silently to the right. There were seven lines of citizens, all in pink masks. One line seemed appreciably shorter and Eric started for it, but Thomas, wise in the ways of bureaucracy, steered them toward the longest line of some twenty citizens. There, they shuffled for forty-five minutes. When there was only one good citizen between them and a clerk, Eric noted that the short line had indeed not moved at all, that the eight citizens in it were now leaning on one another with their pink masks off and their mouths opened to pant.

The clerk looked up when Thomas and Eric bumped shoulders to step forward. "Only one at a time," the clerk hissed, removing her mask. Patches of cotton stuck to her cheeks where long red, indented bands stretched to her pink, fat ears.

"We're here together," Eric said.

"One. At. A. Time."

Since Thomas stood closest, Eric passed him the *Get Out of Jail Free!* card.

The clerk took it, held it to the light, sniffed it, and then turned to an ultra-violet scanner.

"Good. No watermark. Stupid counterfeiters make the mistake of etching in a watermark, some stupid seal they think will work. But there's not supposed to be one. Good. Just one more test." The clerk stuck out her tongue and licked the card. "Yes, cat urine. This card is valid. No one ever can duplicate that. There's never been a counterfeit card. Never, ever, never."

Eric thought there was a flaw in the clerk's logic, but flaws were typical of bureaucracy, so he let the matter go. Besides, he didn't want her to call security if he spoke out of turn.

"Just who is it that you wish to relieve from our fine jail?"

"The woman you just brought in. Teresa Cox."

The clerk's face fell. "Number 314? Don't you have someone else you want to get out?"

"She's my sister."

"And my... fiancé," Eric blurted.

"One. At. A. Time. Do I need to call security?"

Thomas stepped back on Eric's foot, and Eric yelped.

The clerk gave a tsk and shake of her head. "This is going to really upset the tank commanders. They were so proud to bring in Number 314 in such a prompt fashion, three days ahead of schedule. Wouldn't you prefer to release the half? They haven't brought him or her in, but I'm certain he or she would be relieved to get sprung."

"Teresa Cox," Thomas stated. "Number 314."

With a sigh, the clerk passed back the card and indicated a dark double door to her right, their left. She put up a sign indicating lunch break and smiled at Eric.

Eric smiled back, which befuddled the clerk.

"Sir!" the clerk shouted when Eric moved toward the door with Thomas.

Eric simply pointed at the lunch break sign. The clerk shrugged, straightened the sign, and walked away. The twenty-two citizens who'd stood behind Eric cursed.

Eric and Thomas entered the door after showing the *Get Out of Jail Free!* card to the matron guarding it, shifting from buttock to buttock and slapping a Taser on her left palm.

Another long corridor. The sound of every step they took was magnified. It was as if they wore tap-dancing shoes. Eric counted 98 heel-toe clicking steps until they reached the door at the end of the corridor. It was stainless steel and no one was guarding it. The door opened silently inward as they approached.

Another matron was seated inside behind a teller's cage. She briefly looked at them over the *Invisible Woman* comic book in her hands and then returned to reading, her eyes alternating between hooded with somber peace and opened with frantic alarm. A bench nearby looked inviting. There was even an almond-coconut Mounds bar lying unopened on it.

When Eric started for it, the woman said, "That's my break snack." He stopped and stood at attention beside Thomas while the woman continued to read.

"I go on break in a moment," she said, looking over the comic. "So you'll need to sit and wait. Could you hand me that Mounds bar?" Eric did. She returned to the comic, and they sat. Eric let out a sigh, but Thomas grabbed his arm and put his finger to his mouth.

The woman snickered at something. They leaned to see her put down the comic, stand, and scratch her elbows. She opened the candy bar and turned away. Eric watched her jaws working. A digital clock with pink numerals clicked. Eric vaguely wondered how they'd gotten a digital clock to click out seconds. He watched Thomas tap his fingers on his thigh and nod seriously, as if he were a conductor and the clicking clock a fine musical instrument preserved from the Renaissance. Tchaikovsky? Snoop Dog Snoop? It was hard to tell what the beat was.

"Next," the woman intoned, though they were the only ones in the small room. She swallowed the last of her Mounds bar and stretched her neck, which gave off a pop.

Standing before her they showed her the *Get Out of Jail Free!* card. She mumbled and placed it in some type of scanner, tapping her nails exactly as Thomas had tapped his fingers. At last, when the scanner spit the card out, she seemed satisfied. "It's sterile in here. We keep it that way. You can take off those masks. The judge will see you," she said. "Soon enough," she added. "Soon enough." She indicated a double set of mahogany doors, whose doors also slowly opened inward as they approached.

A man behind an elevated mahogany desk busied himself reading papers, shuffling them, and rasping noisily.

"All rise!" a disembodied voice sounded.

Eric and Thomas looked at one another.

"He means that we should sit first," Thomas whispered, being accustomed to the arcane ways of the courtroom. "So that we can then rise." Thomas tilted his head. "But I don't think that's the judge behind that desk," he whispered again as they sat in the sole pew available. "It may be the pre-judge-judge."

When the man behind the desk coughed, Thomas nudged Eric's elbow, and they stood.

"You may be seated," the disembodied voice said.

Other than that single cough, the man behind the desk had not stopped shuffling his papers.

"Docket Two, Case four-hundred-fifteen," the voice said.

Eric thought that maybe the voice was coming from a hardback chair to the left of the grand desk. An implanted speaker? A talking chair-oid?

The man behind the desk looked up. He gave a brisk motion with his right hand as if swatting at a mosquito that had flown near his nose.

Thomas nudged Eric's elbow, and they walked forward to stand before the huge desk and look up. Eric shuffled, feeling he should have had a moist, limp cap to pleat and hold in his hands to indicate humility. The desk was elevated two feet. He and Thomas would have to stand side-by-side and extend their arms to cover even one-half of the desk's width. Already, his neck was sore from looking up.

The man behind the desk gave another brisk motion, with his left hand this time, and Eric handed him the card, having to hop to get it to him. The man put on a pair of glasses and turned the card about, looking at it upside down. Then he turned it about and studied the blank yellow back. He flicked it and studied the edge, putting it to his ear for another flick.

"You may go on in," he finally said, flipping the card back to them. Eric lunged to catch it.

If the pre-judge's desk extended in an airplane's wings, the judge's desk extended for an entire mahogany landing strip. And it was elevated three feet in the air. Eric and Thomas craned their necks to see the man seated behind it. Eric felt his muscles tightening, his breath constricting. The man pushed a small brass placard forward. *Keep calm and breathe evenly.* He tapped the placard and withdrew it.

The law's paw, someone had scratched on the mahogany directly before them, at eye-height.

His Honorable Horror, someone else had knifed into the wood to the left of the first inscription.

Anti-Tanks, the bottom line, —T. It appeared that this was scratched in with a straight pin. There were blood splotches around it, not quite dried. It was lower than the others, about Teresa's height when she was kicking the Vitality Dance.

Eric pointed it out to Thomas, who gave a small grunt.

"Eh? Don't talk while I'm reading. Didn't you see my little plaque?" the judge behind the huge desk gave out a hiss. He shuffled more papers and coughed.

"Docket Three, Case four-hundred-fifteen," the voice repeated.

Thomas made to hand the judge the *Get Out of Jail Free!* card, but the judge waved it off and picked up a piece of paper to read. He smiled grandly. "Ho-ho-ho. *This* is going to make some tankers mighty unhappy." He slammed down a gavel, and Eric's shoulder bones quivered. The sound echoed throughout the chamber, which now that Eric turned to focus on something other than the huge desk, sprawled equally huge and dark.

"Bailiff, release number 314 to the custody of these two fine citizens. Immediately."

The empty chair shuffled toward the back of the courtroom, scraping the floor. So it was a chair-oid after all. The Green-Life-First Party could be proud.

A side door opened. A short, almost dwarf-sized Lieutenant Riley led Teresa into the room, giving her rear end and shoulder a slap and a squeeze and pushing her toward Eric.

57. TERESA AND ERIC AT HOME.

I don't want to forget!" Teresa shouted.

Eric had just suggested they return to see Teresa the Counselor. Thomas had also urged she do that same thing moments before he had to leave. PuckPooch remained neutral.

"You know what?" Teresa said, looking at Eric. "This is it, the camel that stepped on the straw. From now on, I'm going to do more than keep books! I'm going to be the one that crawls over the turret and inserts the Styrofoam in the barrel." Teresa bent and took two creep-crawl two steps in the sexy manner that Eric always envisioned. He was momentarily taken aback. Teresa straightened. "I'm going to learn to mix the Super Express Glue." She stirred vigorously until she panted. "I'm going to carry the kerosene and the weighted socks and throw them over the cameras!" As Teresa made motion with both hands to slam a black sock over a tank's camera, she stopped and looked at Eric, her lips trembling.

"They kept calling me Lucky 314. I didn't know what it meant, but I did know it wasn't good. How did you and Thomas ever bail me out?"

"You're not bailed out. You're completely free!"

"But how?"

Eric shrugged and said, "A yellow *Get Out of Jail Free!* card."

Teresa half-laughed, half-spit. "What? Did it have an old white guy in a top hat with a cane and wings?"

Eric blinked, remembering the card. "Yeah, I think it did. Why?"

Teresa burst out an expletive that neither Eric nor PuckPooch understood. She ran to the bedroom and opened the trunk she'd moved from her apartment. Eric and PuckPooch followed to the foot of their bed. She dug around, tossed PuckPooch an old scarf, which he shook, and then she pulled out a *Monopoly* game.

"Look familiar?" she asked.

Eric shook his head. "My parents wouldn't even play cards. We did have a piano and a cat, though."

Teresa bent to touch the floor. "That's a pretty low bottom line, Eric."

"I know, I know."

She found the yellow *Get Out of Jail Free!* card and handed it to Eric, who flicked it and gave it a sniff. "I don't think it's real."

"How can it not be real, Eric? What does that mean?"

"I don't think it tastes like cat urine."

"You don't *think*?"

"That was one of the very last tests. A clerk licked it and made a face and confirmed the card was real because it tasted like cat urine."

"Who would ever be sick enough to know what cat urine tastes like?"

They both looked to PuckPooch.

Teresa took the card from Eric and held it out to PuckPooch, who gave a sniff and turned aside.

"See, I told you. It's not real. I still have the real card in my wallet. They punched it and gave it back. It's only good for one use."

Teresa twittered her right hand, and Eric retrieved the card. She compared it to the one from the Monopoly set. They looked identical. She held the new card out to PuckPooch, who began to sniff and push at it with his nose, giving it a vigorous lick.

"See?" Eric said.

Teresa held the cards up to the ceiling light. "Yes! *This* is how we'll bring down the tankers," she exclaimed.

"The clerk said that counterfeiters try all the time and it never works."

Teresa jutted her jaw and shoved her head forward. "How would they know it didn't work? If it worked, they wouldn't know, now would they?"

"That's what I thought, too. But I couldn't speak since I was technically still in line behind your brother."

Teresa made a squinty face. "Anyway, I'm not talking about counterfeiting; I'm talking about the bottom line." When she bent the way Eric loved, he swooned.

58. THE NEW BOTTOM LINE.

We're going to get my brother to sue."

"Sue who?"

"Everyone. The state, the city, the nation, The Pink Man. We're going to bring a class-action suit on behalf of the good citizens and Hasbro, or whoever owns the trademark and copyright to *Monopoly*. And we're going to donate the victory proceeds to poor people."

"Can we give some to the SPCA?"

Eric and Teresa looked to PuckPooch, who gave a sniff at a rawhide chewie and started gnawing.

When Teresa called her brother, he was excited. This could be the big case that broke the ceiling for him. This could be the big case that set him amongst the legal eagle immortals, Clarence Darrow, Archibald Cox, Rudy Giuliani. He promised to call back after noon and do some investigating.

They went to the Starbucks magteria to celebrate, taking PuckPooch along with them. "You can't trick me anymore," the barista sang when they approached the counter. "I saw your dog eating one of our sausage biscuits last week." The barista gave a wink. "But since Sacred Splinter Day is just around the corner, I'll let it go." She turned to fix their order and looked back. "Just imagine: Both popes, the Dali Llama, seven imams, fourteen rabbis, and The Mormon Tabernacle Choir. All to listen to The Pink Man, who has promised a moral surprise."

Eric coughed loudly at the word, *moral.* Only phlegm came up. He only momentarily thought this symbolic.

The machine behind the barista whirred, and PuckPooch thumped his tail against a chair. Eric searched hard, just in case a moral *might* show up, leaning against a chair leg or coiled along an electric cord.

The barista brought their two drinks and gave them a saucer of cream for PuckPooch. She took their payment of thirty-two Pinkers and leaned across the counter. "I shouldn't be telling you this, but my cousin works at Precinct Eight and he says—and he's a lieutenant there—he says The Pink Man is going to pardon 314 prisoners if they promise to take the Spirit to their hearts. Isn't that grand? I wouldn't miss it for the world. I have the day off. Are you two—" she leaned to watch PuckPooch lap the cream—"are you *three* going?"

"We hadn't..."

"Yes," Teresa said, grabbing Eric's arm. "We also wouldn't miss it for the world." She tilted her head at Eric and mouthed, "A moral."

59. BAD NEWS AGGLOMERATES.

It's too bad, sis. I thought you really had something. I'm sorry. Keep on thinking that way, though. Something will pop up. Hey, guess what? I've actually got a date. She's another lawyer, so we understand time constraints and all. We're going to attend The Sacred Splinter Day celebration." There was a pause on the phone. "Well, aren't you going to congratulate me, sis?"

Teresa had already handed the phone to Eric and slumped on the floor.

"Sure, sure, Thomas. Teresa just sat down and handed me the phone. Hey, what's the lucky woman's name?"

"You're not going to believe this, Eric, but it's Teresa. She may spell it with an *H*, but I'm not sure."

What Thomas had told Teresa without an *H* that sent her to the floor was that The Pink Man had bought out Hasbro two years ago, the entire corporation. And anyway, the copyright on *Monopoly* had expired a year back. So no class-action lawsuit.

60. A DREAM.

I had the strangest dream," Eric told Teresa and PuckPooch, who both turned attentively, eager for good news after what Thomas had told them the day before.

"A dump truck pulled to our front door and emptied out—not a million Pinkers, but a million ten-centers."

"So we weren't millionaires, but hundred thousand-aires?"

Eric nodded. "And in my dream, you, PuckPooch, could have all the real dog biscuits you want—no more honey baked, oregano infused."

PuckPooch thumped his tail.

"I think my dream's a good omen for Sacred Splinter Day," Eric added.

"Yes," Teresa agreed. "Let's hope so anyway. And maybe Thomas's Theresa will be the light of his life."

"Just like you are for mine," Eric asserted.

PuckPooch thumped his tail happily, but Teresa just stirred her tea. She still had not recovered from Thomas's bad news about Monopoly.

61. THE NUMBER RE-ACHIEVED.

Teresa had not returned to her apartment. Her lease ran out, and the landlord rented it to a newly wedded Mexican couple. Three days later, tankers caught the bride out in the open, sitting on the bench in a yoga pose, watching the sunrise.

So, at 23 years old, Maria Olivia Arguelles became the new number 314.

62. THE ANTI-TANKERS NON-PLAN PLAN.

It was Teresa who spoke loudest at the anti-tanker meeting. Eric stood proudly by her side.

"There are going to be children there. Many, many, many children. Innocence must mean something to us and to the world. Mustn't it?"

Antoinette snorted softly, but even she wrapped her blue scarf about her neck and bowed her head. The vote was unanimous: there would be no protests, no confrontations on Sacred Splinter Day.

63. SACRED SPLINTER DAY ARRIVES.

Winter solstice, the shortest day of the year. Everyone in the city, in the state, in the nation, buzzed about the irony of that since the very best moral ever, the goodest patriotic and spiritual news ever, was being unveiled and celebrated on this very day.

"Thomas," Teresa said, walking up to her brother, who had agreed to meet her and Eric at a small Starbucks kiosk on Nineteenth Street.

Hearing her, both Eric and Thomas lurched spasmodically, for Teresa had gotten her brother's name right. Maybe Sacred Splinter Day really would hold wonders.

Thomas looked chipper. He was chewing gum and not a cigar. He smiled that grand smile of his and said, "Teresa, Eric, great to see you both. I'd like you to meet my sometimes legal opponent but always friend, Theresa Riley."

Eric looked into the hazel eyes of the tall woman before him. Ash hair and a plenteous figure... and could it be, yes, it was: cinnamon.

Thomas grinned. "See a similarity? She's Lieutenant Riley's younger sister. We met years ago when I got him off that triple Murder-One charge."

"And it's taken your brother this long to get around to going out with me on a date—outside the courtroom, that is." When Theresa Riley said this, his Teresa actually smiled, Eric noted. Theresa Riley turned to look at PuckPooch, who, true to form, wagged his tail to greet a stranger. This new Theresa bent to pet him. "He's real! What a delight."

Eric and Teresa hushed her, for they had told this barista that PuckPooch was a dog-oid. "And when he begs for a bite of your doughnut, don't give it to him in here," Teresa said, still smiling, leaning conspiratorially to Theresa Riley.

Donut, the magic word, even though this shop had none because of the sugar shortage. Eric and Thomas exchanged happy glances. The counselor's work had worked. They sat to chat. Teresa was younger than Theresa. Or was she older? It didn't matter, for they both began to get on famously.

Thomas wore an alarm watch that buzzed some twenty minutes later. "I have a surprise for you two," he announced. "Theresa here arranged for extra tickets, and we all are going to be watching from the stands near the Sacred Splinter."

"My brother, your boss, got them for me," Theresa Riley said proudly.

Eric wondered, *Could the cinnamon smell be genetic? Crossover hormones, maybe?*

"Let's finish up, we need to get moving," Thomas said.

"Let me order a doughnut—I mean a biscuit—to take along for PuckPooch." Teresa stood and placed the order, coming back with a bag that looked as if it had more than one biscuit for one dog. Eric smiled grandly. At last, she'd gain some weight. No hanging clothes, no worries about osteoporosis.

The walk to the stands took twelve minutes according to Eric's watch, which had a timer too. Everyone who was anyone had a timer on his watch to make appointments in a—yes, timely manner. And Eric could check his pulse. He could check Teresa's pulse. He could even check PuckPooch's pulse. The watch had no truth meter, though, and Eric did find this disturbing, for it could assess no moral.

Their seats, it turned out, were quite VIP: they were on the very end of the first and second rows facing the green that was to hold—to 'cradle' in the current PR parlance—the Sacred Splinter. The Space Corps Band members were assembling on the green, and the Mormon Tabernacle Choir was donning their robes. PuckPooch gave a low whine and twisting sniff. Aha! The Special Needs Turkey sat in a cage not fifty yards from where they sat.

"My brother said you guys should sit in the front row. He said us lawyers hog all the privileges and should take a back seat now and then."

"Who are those folk?" Teresa asked as she sat, pointing to a group of fifty or so who lingered on the edge of the green, under some elm trees, keeping separate from all the others and the turkey. Some of the group turned her way as if they miraculously heard her query over that distance.

"I think they're connected to the Space Corps," Theresa Riley replied. "My brother said they'd be here too. Maybe a color guard? With those sparkly laser rifles, I mean."

Both Teresa and Eric tried to remember the last time they'd seen these people. All either could pull up, though, was the taste of coconut and raspberry.

Fifteen minutes later, the Space Corps Band started playing. On a distant building a *pop!* sounded to draw their attention when a widescreen monitor lit. As messages and advertisements scrolled and changed on the monitor, the Space Corps Band's brass section initiated a heraldic four-note blow.

"WELCOME!"

Bldl-ut-ta-da!

"SACRED SPLINTER DAY!"

Bldl-ut-ta-da!

"POPE FELIX IV!"

Bldl-ut-ta-da!

With this last trumpet blast, a popemobile stopped before the stands.

"POPE BUDDY I!"

Bldl-ut-ta-da!

A second popemobile stopped before the stands.

"POP TARTS HAVE PROTEIN!"

Bldl-ut-ta-da!

"HIS EXCELLENCY THE DALAI LAMA!"

Bldl-ut-ta-da!

A man in a yellow robe ambled forward and bowed.

"RICE CRISPIES! START YOUR DAY WITH A CRACKLE!"

Bldl-ut-ta-da!

Fourteen rabbis were announced on the monitor. Six ayatollahs were announced. Seven Swamis were announced. Each arrived in a variously colored mobile resembling an old Volkswagen with its roof cut out. Each waved and exited to a platform before the stands where Eric and Teresa sat.

THE MOST HONORABLE PINK MAN!

Drums began furiously tat-tatting and rolling. The Pinkmobile drove up, and The Pink Man, enjoined by two scantily clad blonde women, waved and then exited. He did not go onstage, though. Instead, he turned expectantly to where a carriage drawn by twelve white horses clomped forward.

"THE SACRED SPLINTER!"

The entire band and the Mormon Tabernacle Choir sent up a cacophony that frightened every pigeon and crow within a half mile. Six members of the Space Corps marched to the carriage when the horses clip-clopped to a stop. One horse snorted. One of The Pink Man's aides on his right took its picture. The Space Corps' six members saluted The Pink Man. After he nodded, they turned and lifted a bier off the carriage. Ensconced upon pink cushions was a foot-long shaft of wood. They removed the bier and sat it upon the street.

An old green and yellow pick-up truck followed behind, blowing exhaust as if to prove it was of the people. On the side of the truck was painted in red and yellow, *Abe's Antiques*. A dark-haired man with a goatee got out, slammed the truck's door, and bowed to The Pink Man, who nodded formally.

"ABE JOHNSON!"

Bldl-ut-ta-da!

The man named Abe Johnson wielded a spectacularly oversized magnifying glass. He walked up to the sacred splinter. He sniffed it. As he did, Eric leaned back to whiff at Theresa Riley, getting what he expected: cinnamon.

Abe Johnson was wearing pink latex examination gloves. He rubbed his left hand over the foot-long splinter, sniffed it again, and then looked to the sky, which showed a spectacular clear and cold blue. Then he swept the magnifying glass over the Sacred Splinter, making several passes. He nodded somberly and walked to a microphone that had been placed near the Pink Man. Abe bowed to The Pink Man, waved his oversized magnifying glass, which caught a bit of sunlight and started leaves smoldering by The Pink Man's left shoe.

"Real," Abe said, his voice echoing with amplification to the surrounding crowd and off the surrounding buildings. "Lebanon Cedar from 33 B.C. It is consummated."

The Pink Man clapped. Those in the stands clapped. Those on the platform clapped. The two announcers from the TV broadcast clapped. All the nation clapped as it viewed this miracle on podcasts and networks.

"W.W.J.D. A NEW SONG FOR A NEW DAWN!"

Bldl-ut-ta-da!

The Space Corps Band started up, to be joined by the Mormon Tabernacle Choir, who sang, as the monitor scrolled out the lyrics,

"THOUGH HIS TIMES WERE DIFFERENT,
FOR HE HAD NO DRUGS NOR GUNS,
BABY JESUS BECAME THE MAN
WHO TURNED THAT DARK INTO A SUN.
THIS ONE ETERNAL TRUTH WE TURN TO:
WHAT, OH, WHAT WOULD JESUS HAVE DONES?"

The Pink Man appeared to bow reverently at the song's end, though he may have simply been straightening a crick in his neck. Then he turned to the Space Corps Color Guard and gave a nod.

Quickly enough, Eric and Teresa's memory returned.

64. A MEMORY JARRED, A NEW MEMORY MADE.

How had the three hundred and thirteen traitors been shuffled into a corral on the edge of the green so quickly? Had everyone been paying attention to Abe the Antique dealer and his giant magnifying glass? Had everyone leaned forward in terror or anticipation at the smoldering leaves by The Pink Man's left shoe? Was there a Klingon cloaking device?

And why were there only three hundred and thirteen traitors? Why weren't there three hundred and fourteen? Because the newly wedded Mexican bride had hung herself in the prison the previous night after being raped by three guards. That is why.

The Space Corps Firing Squad, for of course they were not a color guard, assembled briskly.

The Pink Man was once more handed a pink card by Captain—now Major—Carmel.

The Pink Man read two verses from Psalm 9. "For thou hast maintained my right and my cause; thou sattest in the throne judging right. / Thou hast rebuked the heathen, thou hast destroyed the wicked, thou hast put out their name for ever and ever."

These were new, improved laser rifles, automatically firing fifteen bursts per minute. Fifteen times forty-nine cracks cracked. 313 prisoners within the corral fell, receiving an average of 2.34 laser bursts apiece. The fiftieth rifleman— the one especially picked by Major Carmel for his previous prowess, turned to the stands to quickly fire just two bursts.

But PuckPooch was quicker. He jumped and knocked both Eric and Teresa over. The laser bolts hit the two onlookers directly behind them: Thomas Cox and Theresa Riley. Theresa had the honor of being the half. Thomas, number 314, was quite dead.

65. The Moral.

They stayed inside for three days, not going to work, not calling in. They sat before the TV, surfing channels. Every time a sitcom or a game show or a soap or a movie came on, they flipped to another channel, in search of commercials. Commercials offered the best chance of finding a moral, they'd decided, for commercials were something people cared about. Commercials moved the nation, they moved the folk. Commercials offered an artery to life. Commercials got the goods.

And whenever either Eric or Teresa lapsed into a weak and nauseated state and let the remote control drop with a tired plop onto the couch, the other would pick it up and rapidly flick the channels in search of The One True Commercial. This, though they had decided in unspoken yet uplifting hope that there might actually be *more* than One True Commercial. Two, even three. It was possible, was it not?

PuckPooch whined incessantly during those first three days. On the fourth he became so disillusioned that he turned into a dog-oid. Every evening afterward, at sunset, which came one minute later every evening because of the passing of the winter solstice, his newly discovered computer chip would cause him to bark, and one of them would stand and lead him to an electrical outlet to be charged. On one such sunset, Teresa had assiduously palpated her own rear end to see if there might be an electrical connection so that she, too, could plug in. There was not. On one such sunset, Eric had similarly palpated his hamhocks to see if there might be an electrical connection so he, too, could plug in. There was not. Neither mentioned this fervent search, this fervent androidal hope, to the other.

When PuckPooch barked that electrical way, they would also place a frozen dinner in the microwave. One *Ding!* and eight minutes later, they would split it. A stack of dinners perched in the freezer, too many to count. A stack of spent plastic trays mounted in the garbage can, too many to count. Every seventeen minutes, PuckPooch's tail would thump. They'd lift their heads at the noise. Surely, they thought, a moral will show before the thumps and the frozen dinners run out, before the garbage spills, before the electricity is cut off, before the eviction notice... Surely.

Scientific American praised the advent of the automatic laser rifle and its humane efficiency.

Mother Earth News remained happy to see that the Terrific Tom was still gobbling but warned the nation must not let its guard down against GMOs.

Harper's thought that perhaps Walt Whitman would have been given pause at all the death on Sacred Splinter Day. The magazine wondered if he might have tramped onto the field or into the stands as a Wound Dresser.

The New Yorker was not able to publish its Splinter Day issue due to multiple problems with ink and paper shortages, a lunker's union strike, the derailment of several trains, and a prolonged electrical outage in its building.

Washington Post praised The Pink Man's courage, his decisiveness, and his spiritual stance as evinced by his sober reading of Psalm 9.

L. A. Times stated that, for once, its editor had caved into the East and its over-bearing time zone issue and had flown to the capitol, taking his entire family, a wife and two daughters. That editor wrote, "The four of us were even able to sit down to a pleasant steak dinner after the Sacred Splinter Celebration."

Tuscaloosa News stated that a record eleventh five-star recruit had been added. Next year's team would be a clear preseason number one.

THE END

ABOUT THE AUTHOR

Joe Taylor has had several novels published, most recently *The Theoretics of Love* from New South Books and *Back to the Wine Jug* from Sagging Meniscus Press. He's also had some story collections published, most recently *Ghostly Demarcations*. He has two novels in verse published: *Pineapple* and *Back to the Wine Jug*, and a mixed-form novel entitled *Highway 28 West*. He and Tricia have ten dogs and three cats—so don't drop any more off! He has been the director of Livingston Press at the University of West Alabama... forever.

Made in USA - Kendallville, IN
25445_9798345422236
11.30.2024 2015